YOU COULD DIE LAUGHING
or
I Was A Comic For The F.B.I.

THE SWINGERS

BOOKS BY JOEY ADAMS

GAGS TO RICHES
THE CURTAIN NEVER FALLS
JOEY ADAMS JOKE BOOK
STRICTLY FOR LAUGHS
IT TAKES ONE TO KNOW ONE
JOEY ADAMS JOKE DICTIONARY
CINDY AND I
ON THE ROAD FOR UNCLE SAM
JOEY ADAMS' ROUND THE WORLD JOKE BOOK
L. B. J. TEXAS LAUGHS
HOW TO MAKE AND TELL JOKES FOR ALL OCCASIONS
THE BORSCHT BELT

You Could Die Laughing

or

I Was A Comic For The F.B.I.

and

THE SWINGERS

By JOEY ADAMS

THE BOBBS-MERRILL COMPANY, INC.
Indianapolis · New York

The Bobbs-Merrill Company, Inc.
A Subsidiary of Howard W. Sams & Co., Inc., Publishers
Indianapolis · Kansas City · New York

CONTENTS

You Could Die Laughing

or

I Was A Comic For The F.B.I.

CHARLIE Davis is the greatest comic in show-business. And I should know, he's told it to me often enough. He also is the greatest director, actor, and producer we have in the business today. That's all admitted. Of course, he's the one who admits it.

The funny part of it is, he's not far wrong. His pictures and TV shows have made millions for him as well as every-body around him, including Star Pictures and the International Network. Recently he made world news off the theatrical pages. He would be telling you this story himself, but he is a little modest about it, and furthermore, reading and writing aren't exactly his forte. So he asked me to write this down for him.

You see, while most of us were learning the three Rs, he was learning the buck and wing. While we were playing with rattles, he was playing with greasepaint. Charlie's mother and dad were vaudeville hoofers who brought him up on punch lines. His playpen was the backstage dressing rooms in every broken-down vaudeville theater in the country. His schooling was strictly the hard-knock variety. His teachers were the greatest in the world—the vaudeville performers on the Dow, Keith, Pantages and Loew's time. How else could one poor skinny little kid without formal education go from gags to riches in one short generation?

It was a pleasure to watch him operate. More like a work of art. Take the night this story began. It started out as an ordinary Davis night. It was about twelve midnight when he parked his white convertible Rolls-Royce in front of the Stage Delicatessen—doesn't everybody?—and strolled into the restaurant. He spotted me at the front table sitting with Max Asnas, the Sage of the Stage, better known as the corned-beef Confucius. "I hear you had a fire here, Max," he opened, "the first time the food has been hot in your place in twenty years."

"What are you looking for," Max asked, "a sandwich or an audience?"

"I'd eat here," he stabbed, "but I don't need heartburn."

"What do you expect in a delicatessen—sunburn?" Max answered.

But Charlie wasn't listening. He had his hand on my shoulder and was looking around as he spoke to me. "How's everything, Kid?" he wanted to know. Meanwhile, he was surveying the room in case there was somebody more important than me to sit with. Maybe a columnist or a Bob Hope or somebody. On the other hand, he didn't want to lose me if I turned out to be the best bet in the room at the time.

"Oh," I said, knowing he never hears you, "things haven't been too good. My brother died, my mother and father are very ill, my sister is in the hospital and I was hit by a truck."

"That's fine, Kid," he said without listening. "Glad to hear it."

"Not only that," I added, "but the Commies have taken over and it looks like war."

"Happy to hear it," he said, patting me on the shoulder as he continued casing the room. "Well, it looks like you won me," Charlie said to Max as he sat down at our table. "I'm your guest."

"I'm putting you down on my Income Tax with my two other dead deductions—my wife and the race track," Max answered.

You don't have to worry about insulting Charlie. He doesn't hear anything but compliments—even if he has to throw them himself. Naturally, he started off talking about his new show and stayed that way.

After a half-hour of a Charlie Davis eulogy, Max interrupted. "I don't want to take you off your favorite subject," he said to Charlie, "but all you do is talk about yourself. How about talking about me for a change?"

"Okay," Charlie said, "what do *you* think about *my* show?"

When the check came it was the perfect cue for Davis to make his exit. It is a well-known fact that Charlie gets a slight impediment of the reach when the tab arrives. It's the fastest way to get rid of him when the I-strain gets a bit too much.

It was about 1:30 A.M. when Charlie got into his shiny white Rolls-Royce and drove away. That is, he fumbled with the door a little, coughed a lot, signed a few autographs, and when he was sure everybody in the neighborhood saw him get into the Rolls, he then drove away into the night, after he played the exhaust for a minute or two, of course.

Charlie headed for El Morocco. To Charlie it was the shank of the evening. Still a couple of hours left to take some bows before he turned in. He headed east on 54th Street in a leisurely manner. He was stopped by a red light on Third Avenue when the telephone rang. "Hold on a minute," Charlie ad-libbed as he picked up the instrument, "I'm on the other phone." Isn't he beautiful?

"I'm a big fan of yours," the female voice on the other end cooed. "I must see you—it's important."

"Every broad in town wants to see me," Charlie gagged. "My price is very cheap. Just a couple of ties."

"This is no laughing matter, Mr. Davis," she said solemnly. "I saw them throw that man into the back of your car while you were in the Stage."

"What man?" he hollered as he turned around. The body was stretched out on the floor of the car like he was asleep. Even in the dark he could see the hole where his right eye used to be. Charlie froze.

"Mr. Davis—Mr. Davis," the voice kept squawking through the receiver—"Mr. Davis, are you there?" The cars were honking noisily in back of him trying to move on the green. Finally, he put his foot on the accelerator and started to move slowly forward. The phone was still in his hand. "Mr. Davis—are you there?" she kept saying over and over.

"Yes," he whispered. "Who is this man? Who are you?"

"I told you," she said, "I'm a fan of yours. I saw them pull up in a car right next to yours, open your door and dump him in—"

"Who is them?" Charlie spoke quickly into the phone.

"I don't know. Two men I never saw before."

"How did you get my number?" Charlie asked.

"It's easy," she answered. "I called Information and she told me to call long distance and ask for the mobile service operator. I invested a fast thirty cents and here I am."

"It's a lucky thing I'm listed," he said into the phone. Lucky? As if Charlie Davis would miss any kind of billing, even in a mobile telephone book. "Anyway," he continued, "thanks for telling me. Where are you? Can I see you? Can you meet me now?"

"What do you think I have been trying to tell you? Sure I can meet you. Pick me up at Fifty-fifth Street and Broadway. The southeast corner. You can't miss me. I'm blonde and adorable," she cooed, "and I'll be waiting."

Talk about mixed emotions. What do you do first? A sultry-sounding blonde waiting on a dark corner and a dead body waiting in the back of your car. Naturally, he went to see the blonde—and took the body with him. Anyway, the man wasn't going to run away and the blonde might.

Naturally, Charlie fell in love as soon as the blonde got into the Rolls and sat down next to him. After all, she was his type—a girl—about $46 \times 24 \times 36$ and available now. "My name," she crooned, "is Candy Sweets. My friends call me Sugar."

"Okay, Sugar," he said, "now tell me. Why are you doing all this for me? Why did you call me and tell me about the body?"

"I told you," she said, "I'm your fan. I've been watching you for years but this is the first time I've had a chance to talk to you in person."

"How did you know it was my car?" he asked. "I mean, how come you saw it all—I mean, what were you doing on the street by yourself at one-thirty?"

"Look, pal," she told him, "Seventh Avenue is my beat. I've been working this street for years. I know everything that goes on here. As I was walking along I noticed your car. It ain't exactly inconspicuous, you know. Everybody knows your white Rolls. Anyway, I just happened to be staring at it when this car pulls up alongside it. Two men drag this body out and dump him in your car and drive away. It took a couple of seconds. It's just that I happened to be watching your car—you know, admiring it. Well, anyway, I went to the phone booth on the corner, called the operator, got your number, then watched for you to come out of the Stage and called you. That's the whole story."

"Gee, thanks," he mumbled. "But why me? I don't even know the guy. Do you?"

She turned around and looked down at the body on the

floor. "No," she groaned. "I never saw him before in my life."

"Well," Charlie pleaded, "what do I do now? What do I do with the body?"

"Dump it," she suggested.

"Dump it?"

"Sure—just like they did to you. Pass it on."

"I can't do that," Charlie said. "Suppose somebody sees me—I mean——"

"Well," she persisted, "we can drive to some quiet spot in Central Park. You get in the back of the car. I'll drive. When we get to some secluded spot—just dump him out—"

"But you don't understand," he pleaded. "I should go to the police. I'm legit. I did nothing wrong. I can't afford to get mixed up in this."

"That's just it," she explained. "This gets in the paper and you're ruined. You think your sponsor wants to be connected with dead bodies—right or wrong? Listen to me, I'm on your side. I'm only trying to do what's best for you—dump it—it's the only way out."

After midnight Central Park is like a cemetery with lights. Except for a few cars trickling by and an occasional call for *Help*, it's like a morgue—and now it would have a fresh body to prove it. But at three o'clock in the morning it was so quiet even the muggers were asleep.

Sugar drove around the park twice looking for the right spot to make the deposit. Charlie was sitting hunched down in the back of the Rolls with the body. For the first time in his life, he did not want to be recognized.

"Now," she said as they reached a quiet turn on the west side of the Park at about 95th Street. "Now—open the door—just as I make this turn—I'll stop—just pull him out and dump him in the bushes—fast. . . . Okay? Ready? Now!"

Charlie is one performer who has ice water in his veins.

Nothing makes him nervous. Even before his first big TV show he was air-conditioned. But this was one performance where he wasn't so cool. He was so nervous as he dragged the body out of the car that he didn't even notice the black sedan that passed just as he planted his contraband in the bushes.

"I'll never be able to thank you enough," he said as he got back in the car. "What would I do without you?"

"Fortunately," she answered, "you don't have to. Let's go to my place and celebrate. Do you think you can handle my body without getting nervous?"

"Sure—sure," he said without listening. He was still thinking of the other body. "Sure—anything you say."

Sugar drove the car to the garage in her building on East 54th Street and took the elevator up to 10 C. Charlie collapsed on the couch. It was at least a couple of hours before the old boy really got back into stride. Sugar turned the conversation to his new TV show. Five or six drinks and he was his old modest self again. "It's not definite, baby," he said, "but I may give you my beautiful body—just to show my appreciation—"

"That's very kind of you," Sugar said sweetly.

"Now," he said, "if you're a good girl—"

"Don't worry," she interrupted, "I'll be very good—you're talking to the champ."

When he was getting dressed Charlie suddenly remembered. "Here's the thirty cents you laid out to make that call to me. Nobody will ever say a broad paid for Charlie Davis. And here's a couple of passes to my TV show Saturday," he offered magnanimously.

"That's very sweet of you," she sarcasmed. "I appreciate your giving me your beautiful body and all and your TV show is great and everything, but how do I live? You can't eat passes. What about some bread?"

"Bread?" he hollered. "Bread? You want bread, make love to a baker. I'm an actor—I give passes."

"Bravo," the voice shouted from the doorway. "Bravo, that's telling her, brother."

Charlie stood petrified. He was bent over tying his shoe-lace with his back toward the door. When he heard the voice he froze. For a moment it looked like he would never get up. Slowly he rose and turned around. There were two men standing just inside the bedroom door. One was a tall mus-cular-looking man, blond hair and the longest arms you ever saw. The other was short and stocky. He looked like Edward G. Robinson in one of his early pictures. "Who—who—who are you?" he managed to get out.

"Friends," Edward G. said. "We're with you. We're your fans. We have some pictures of you we'd like you to autograph."

"This is a hell of a time and place to have a meeting of my fan club," Charlie gagged. "It's five o'clock in the morn-ing." The color was beginning to come back into his face—green—and his funny bone came back to life. "Do you al-ways break into apartments looking for autographs?"

"We didn't break in," the blond explained softly. "We were invited," he said, holding up the key. "Isn't that right, Miss Sweets?"

"Did you invite them?" Charlie asked. "Are they friends of yours?"

"Sure," Sugar said nervously, "sure. They said they're fans of yours and wanted to talk to you."

"Wouldn't it be easier just to shake hands?" Charlie asked sarcastically. "How did you know I'd be here at five o'clock in the morning?"

"We arranged it," Edward G. said.

"You mean," Charlie was just coming to, "that this whole thing was a plant just so you could talk to me?"

"Exactly," the blond answered.

"Including the dead body?"

"That's right."

"I don't get it," Charlie said in a funk.

"You will," Edward G. assured him. "Okay, Miss Sweets, you can go now. And thanks for everything," he said as he pressed an envelope into her hand.

Before Charlie could say "A funny thing happened to me on my way to El Morocco," Sugar was out of the apartment and he was left alone with his—fans.

"What has she got to do with this?" Charlie asked.

"Nothing," Edward G. answered. "Nothing at all. Except that she arranged to get you here and set up the pictures. That's all. She knows nothing about our plans or why we're here. We paid her well enough to keep her trap shut."

"Set up what pictures?" Charlie asked, stunned. "What pictures are you talking about? We didn't take any pictures."

"Oh, yes, you did," the blond one said. "And you look beautiful too. Here. Take a look."

Charlie looked down at the half-dozen snapshots the blond pressed into his hands. On top was a picture of Charlie himself dragging a body into the bushes. He gasped. "Where did you get this?" he mumbled. The next pictures showed him in the Rolls with Sugar, going into her apartment building, and in bed with her.

"And I want to tell you," Edward G. said, "you're a hell of a man in the romance department. You should give lessons. Like I said, I'm your fan."

"Never mind the crap," Charlie said. "What's this all about? How did you get these pictures? I never saw anybody taking any pictures."

"I would say you were a little busy with the bodies to notice any flash bulbs going off," Edward G. answered. "First the one in the park and then the one in bed. But I must say you take a great picture. And you should see the others."

"All right," Charlie spit, "I know the jokes. Now what's the pitch? If it's money you want, forget it—I left it all in Vegas."

"We don't want your money," the blond said. "Like we told you—"

"You're my fans, I know. So what's with the frame? What is it you want?"

"We want to help you," the blond said.

"Sure," Charlie answered, "into my grave. These pictures are going to help a lot with my sponsors, let alone my wife—not mentioning the police."

"That's just it," Edward G. interrupted. "We want to keep this out of the papers and out of the wrong hands—"

"Then why the hell did you take them at all? Why this whole setup?"

"Protection. We got to protect ourselves and we got to protect you. For your own good."

"Protect me from what?" Charlie hollered.

"From the same thing happening to you as happened to the guy in the picture. We didn't protect ourselves with him. We didn't think we had to. He was a stanch member of our party. Suddenly he started to make trouble. You know, flipped his lid. So they had to get rid of him. Now, if we had this protection, perhaps we could reason with him and he'd still be alive today. Do you follow me?"

"Sure," Charlie answered. "If I follow you I wind up in the morgue. Now will you stop with this weird dialogue and come to the damn punch line? What are you protecting me from? What is it you want from me?"

"Do you remember doing a benefit for Russian War Relief in 1942?" the blond one asked.

"I don't remember where I was last night," Charlie

answered. "How the hell would I know what I did in 1942?"

"Well, here's a copy of a program that you MC'd for Russian War Relief on August 12, 1942, at the Coronet Theatre. Your name is right on top."

"So what?" Charlie snapped. "I've done benefits for everybody from Cancer to Athlete's Foot. Recently I even helped raise money for a pool table for a group of murderers in a cellar in Brooklyn. I like to do benefits. What's wrong with that?"

"Nothing," Edward G. interrupted quietly, "except this was a communist front organization you worked for. And we know at least six other shows you did for different groups that would be classified as Red."

"Hell," Charlie cried, "I can't investigate every benefit I play. Who the hell remembers what I did in 1942? They didn't even have AGVA or Theatre Authority then to control the benefits. Don't you understand?"

"Oh, we understand all right," Edward G. soothed him, "but will the public understand? Will your sponsors understand? You're guilty by association. You know the newspapers. Once they get hold of a thing like this they never let go. By the time you answer, the boat has sailed and so has your career."

"That's right," the blond added. "This whole country is built on McCarthyism—guilt by association. That's democracy for you. Look here, I'm just as good an American as the next guy. Better. But does that mean we don't see what's wrong? Does that mean we can't improve it?"

Charlie wasn't listening now. He was thinking about the headlines. He remembered the other stars who were painted red and never were heard from again. He remembered how furious he was when he read about that no-good singer Frank Foyle who lost a million-dollar TV career when that book came out with his name in it as a communist collaborator. He wondered now if he wasn't a little too hasty in his judgment of Foyle and the others.

"How did I get mixed up in all this?" he mumbled half aloud. "My whole career—my whole life—just because I did a benefit for a bunch of lousy Reds that I didn't even know I was doing. What do I do now?"

"You don't do anything," the blond one answered calmly. "That is, we'll tell you what to do at the right time. That's why we're here—to protect you—"

"Protect me?" he screamed. "Protect me? Is that why you framed me with that whore and that corpse? Is that why you're threatening me with these Red benefits I was supposed to have done twenty-five years ago? Protect me? You're trying to kill me."

"It's all according to how you look at it," Edward G. answered. "From where we stand we see a great star who could be helpful to us—helpful to our party—helpful to our country. That's the trouble with living in a democracy—anybody can become a whipping boy just because he doesn't agree with the way the politicians and the imperialists are running the country. Our party will eliminate all that—and we want you to help."

"What party?" Charlie asked coldly.

"Why, the communist party, of course," he said, "the party of the people."

"What people? This is the greatest country in the world —and the most prosperous—and you want me to help you louse it up with your dirty Red line? Over my dead body!"

"If that's how you want it," the blond one said solemnly, "it could be arranged. We're trying to save you in spite of yourself. That's the trouble with Americans. They don't know what they want. They need somebody to think for them."

"You mean like framing me to make me do what you want," Charlie said sarcastically.

"If it helps the party—yes!" the blond answered.

"Look," Edward G. interrupted, "we want to protect you even if you don't. We don't want your sponsor to get these pictures. You'd be off the air in seconds. All contracts have morals clauses—you'd be dead. If the papers carried the story of your affiliation with those communist front organizations, you wouldn't get a job in the men's room at the Hilton—"

"Suppose I go to the police and tell them the whole story?" Charlie asked angrily.

"Then *our* story with pictures goes to the Press, the sponsors, and the TV station, as well as your wife—and you go six feet under," he answered. "Anyway, who would believe you? We have the proof—you have nothing!"

"You're forgetting about the blonde—Sugar," Charlie snickered. "She goes for me pretty good, you know."

"She goes for the buck more," Edward G. answered, "and we paid her pretty good—enough for a long trip. Don't worry, you'll never hear from her again."

"You got it all figured out," Charlie grumbled disgustedly. "Heads you win—tails I lose."

"Look," the blond interrupted, "all we want to do is help you, brother Davis—"

"*You* look," Charlie yelled. "Forget the brother stuff—*my* brother is living—and don't give me that crap about wanting to help me. Just tell me what you want me to do."

"If that's the way you want it," the blond said. "But remember we hold all the cards—including the one with your son's address on it. Any questions?"

"You left nothing out—you're right out of a B movie," Charlie spit. "I got a ninety-three-year-old grandmother—

you want her address too? I warn you, *comrades*, if you touch one *hair*—"

"That's up to you," the blond one answered. "Not that you're in any position to warn anybody—"

"Well," Edward G. took over, "now that we all understand each other—"

"Okay," Charlie asked, "what do you want from me?"

"Oh," Edward G. explained, "that will come later. One of our comrades will contact you at your home or the TV station—and I suggest you treat him nicer than you did us —he might not be as understanding as we are."

"Sure," Charlie sneered, "I'll kiss him on the lips. How will I know him—will he be carrying a hammer and sickle?"

"No," Edward G. answered, "he'll be carrying some pictures that I'm sure you'll recognize—and he'll mention the name Sugar. And I suggest you co-operate—this comrade doesn't know from no jokes or temperament. You better convince him you mean business or you're dead. Do I make myself clear?"

"Okay—okay," Charlie grumbled, "I know when I've laid an egg. You made my bed and I gotta lay in it—I'll co-operate with your comrade—I have no choice. But I warn you, if one dirty word gets out about me you'll hear my screams around the world. I'll call the Army, the Navy, the Marines—my Air Raid Warden. I'll——"

"You're one of us now, comrade. We must protect you," Edward G. chimed in. "The bigger you are the better it is for us. Don't worry about a thing—we are ready to die to protect your reputation—"

"Now there's an offer—" Charlie suggested.

"What?"

"Forget it," Charlie said. "I had a great night—but this wasn't it." He looked at his watch. "It's about seven o'clock

in the morning and I have a show tonight. I gotta get some
sleep. I suppose," he said as he walked toward the door,
"I'll be seeing you."

"You won't see us," the blond said. "Another comrade
will contact you from now on."

"And just when I was beginning to get used to you,"
Charlie said. "I'll miss you. Good-bye, Hansel and Gretel—
no regards," he threw at them as he walked out the door.

As soon as he got home he telephoned me. "Did I wake
you?" he asked.

"No—I had to get up to answer the phone anyway," I
yawned.

"Now there's a new line," he heckled.

"What do you expect in the middle of the night—Bob
Hope?"

"What are you doing?" he asked.

"What am I doing?" I yelled. "I'm planting geraniums
in my bathtub." I looked at the clock on my night table.
"What the hell else would I be doing at seven o'clock in the
morning?"

"I must see you immediately," he said seriously. "I got
a part for you in my show tonight and I'd like to talk it over
with you. Can you come over to my apartment right now?"

"You've been on the air for five years and you never
used me once. You finally decide to make me immortal and
this is the only time you could find to call me? You know
Dan Mason isn't exactly a nobody. I've been headlining
night clubs and theaters for years. And I get as good laughs
as anybody. I'm not just a stooge that could be called at—"

"Do you or don't you want the part?" he interrupted
angrily.

"If that's the way you feel about it," I said, "I'll be right
over."

'Star or no star, he isn't going to bulldoze me. If he thinks he can snap his finger and I'll come running just for a part on his TV show—he's right. Anybody takes me for a fool—makes no mistake.' I was doing all the jokes acting as straight man and comic as I showered and got dressed. By the time I reached Charlie's house, about seven minutes later, I was ready to take over his show lock, stock, and gag files.

"The Kid is here," I gagged as he opened the door for me. "You got nothing to worry about now. I'll save your little TV show tonight. Just let me at that audience—"

"If they don't get at you first," he snapped. But his heart wasn't in it. It was just the comic's natural defense attack. Without it you're a straight man. And to a comic, that's like giving him twenty lashes.

"Look," he said, "I need your help. I want you to contact the F.B.I. Do it from a phone booth. Make sure nobody is listening. Tell them to contact me as soon as possible. *And secretly*. Tell them the Commies are forcing me to work for them against my will—"

"Is this a gag?" I asked. "If it is—"

"I wish it were," he said. From the look on his face now I knew he was strictly a straight man. Charlie was in serious trouble. "That's why I called you with that job offer. I'm sure they are following me. My phone might be tapped. These guys mean business. I hate to get you mixed up in this, but if I called the F.B.I. myself I could get very dead very fast. Will you do it? Will you help?"

"Gee, I'm sorry," I said. "Sure. Sure I'll help. What do you want me to do?"

"First call the F.B.I. Remember they may be following you after you leave here, so be careful." I nodded. "Secondly," he continued, "we gotta do a bit on the show tonight. We can't take a chance. In case they were listening or saw you come in here. Can you dig up six good minutes you can do? I'll have my writers work up a bit for us. Will you be at the studio at four o'clock?"

"Anything you say." I tried to console him. "What is it all about? Can you tell me? I mean, how did you get mixed up in this?"

"*I* didn't get mixed up in it. *They* mixed me up—those goddam Reds." He told me the whole story. Exactly as it happened from the time he left me at the Stage Delicatessen until he called me. When he was finished, I just sat there staring. It was at least five minutes before I was able to talk.

"This is America," I mumbled. "We're not in Russia. It can't be. It's gotta be some kind of joke or something."

"I'll tell it to the corpse they dumped in my car—he'll die laughing."

"I don't know what to tell you," I said quietly, "except that I'm proud of you, you hammy bum. You're shooting crap with your life rather than put your country up for sale."

"Look," he said embarrassedly, "I'm no hero. I'm scared stiff. But when I see red, I really blow my top. I don't wanna sound like a square. You know me, who am I kidding? I'd sell my soul for a good belly laugh. But all the money and threats in Russia and China combined couldn't get me to put one hair of Uncle Sam's head on the bargaining table. He's just not for sale."

"You got my vote," I said, trying to break the tension, "but remember I also voted for Barry Goldwater, Wendell Willkie, and Alf Landon."

"How could you vote?" he barked. "You got to pass a literacy test." That's the Charlie Davis I knew and hated. Now he had me all mixed up.

"You're beautiful," I said. "Seriously, I wish the guys could really see you now—I wish they could have heard your speech just now."

"If one word of this gets out, we are all dead—you too. The big thing is no publicity of any kind—nobody must know a thing. Not your wife—brother—sister—anybody. Our lives depend on it, and the lives of so many others. Imagine Charlie Davis fighting to keep his name *out* of the papers—"

"And," I said, "out of the obituary columns. Don't worry, I'll be careful. I'm too young and clever to die."

"Only the F.B.I.," he warned me again. "Not even the police. Nobody. Just call the F.B.I. and talk to one of the agents and tell him to contact me. Don't tell him the whole story. Just the fact that the Reds want me to work for them—that's all. Okay?"

"Okay—and I'll see you at four o'clock rehearsal. Just make sure I get the funny lines. I always thought you'd be my straight man some day."

"And I always thought you'd be a comic some day. We were both wrong," he topped.

"Yeah?" I countered.

"Now there's a clever ad lib," he laughed.

"I don't wanna embarrass you," I said. "Remember, you're older than me."

"And your jokes are older than both of us," he snapped.

Now that I had him in a better mood I decided to leave. And anyway, I couldn't think of a punch line.

I never did get any more sleep. I kept thinking of the unfunny thing that happened to Charlie on his way to his TV show. Furthermore, I had to get my six minutes of hilarious ad libs ready for the show.

When I left his apartment I walked to my place, which is only about eight blocks away. It was the only way I could stop off at a phone booth and make a call without arousing suspicion. If I took a cab it would seem a little funny, if anyone was following me, if I asked the cab to wait and stopped at a street booth to call. Especially since I was on my way home and could call from there. And I remembered that Charlie said to use a public phone.

I felt like 007 but I acted like a square comic. From seeing and reading so many mystery and spy stories I knew that I must not attract any attention or do anything that wasn't normal. I walked about four blocks and then spotted the phone booth on the corner. I nonchalantly walked in, closed the door and dialed the operator and asked her to get me the F.B.I. I asked for the agent in charge and quickly told him the story. Of course he knew Charlie Davis, but I gave him his home address, TV address, and office. As I talked to him I casually looked out of the glass doors to see if anybody was listening or watching. Nobody could overhear me, but just in case anybody was looking my way, I just kept smiling all the time I was talking. I figured that's what James Bond or Perry Mason or Mike Hammer would do.

It was the best show Charlie Davis ever put on the air. Would I lie to you? I was the hit of the show. I had all the funny lines. That is, if you could call "Hello, Charlie" a funny line. Charlie was really upset about his troubles, but not upset enough that he would give me the punch lines and keep the straight lines for himself.

My hilarious six minutes was cut down to a charming two and a half minutes. The big comedy routine that Charlie had promised to write for me turned out to be one straight line. "I think you're the greatest comic in the business," he says. Then I say "You're kidding," and he says "I certainly am." Anyway, they said I was the greatest thing on the show. But who listens to my mother-in-law?

Friendship is one thing and trouble is another. But when Charlie Davis is on stage he forgets everything and everybody. The only thing that counts are those laughs. If you saw him work that night you would think he didn't have a care in the world—or a murder to his name.

To show his friendship to me he let me share his dressing room. Not the laughs or the billing or the loot. Anyway, he hates to be alone and he loves to show off to the other comics. Now he had a special reason for wanting me around as much as possible—I was sharing his burden; not the laughs —just the troubles.

Charlie's phone rang. "Answer it, will you," he asked, "while I take this make-up off? And I don't want to see any fans tonight—"

"Are you kidding?" I heckled. "After your show tonight you have no fans."

"Sure," he topped me again, "with you on the show, I'll have no program either."

"It's some guy from *TV Guide*—wants to interview you. Says he's doing a cover story on you. The doorman wants to know if he should send him up."

"Might as well," he said. "They got eight million readers who love me. I'll give them some instant Charlie Davis and help build their circulation a little."

"Send him up," I said into the phone. "Say a few words about me," I warned Charlie. "I could use the publicity."

"A friend in need," he misquoted, "is a pest."

The man who entered looked like a model for *Gentleman's Quarterly*—vest and all. Only the straw hat pushed back on his head gave him any semblance of a reporter. He took out his credentials and showed them to Charlie. "I'm Don Simon from *TV Guide*," he said. "I'd like to do a story —a cover story—on the serious side of Charlie Davis."

"That's okay," he said to the man. "This is Dan Mason —he's the guy that called you. He's from the F.B.I.," he said to me.

"Glad to know you," I said cleverly, as he showed me his credentials.

"Perhaps it's best," he offered, "if I talk with Mr. Davis

alone. But under no circumstances are you to breathe a word of this to a soul. Does anybody else know about this besides you two?"

"No," I said. "I didn't tell anybody."

"Nobody," Charlie interrupted, "not even my psychiatrist."

"Let's keep it that way," the man said; "your lives may depend on it."

"You've just convinced me," I said as I opened the door and walked out.

"Now," the government man said, "tell me the story, Mr. Davis. Exactly what happened and don't leave any detail out, no matter how small or insignificant it seems to you—I want to hear everything."

And Charlie told him everything. Including the Sugar bit in exquisite detail, the dead body, the pictures, the telephone call to me, my part in the show—everything. Charlie can remember a whole script just by going over it once. Now he was able to recall all the dialogue, including the threats of exposure for his participation in the shows for the Red front organizations and a perfect description of the two Commies.

"Just one thing," Charlie added. "Sugar, that is Candy Sweets, knows nothing about the Red bit. They just used her body and her apartment to get at me. They threw her out before they talked to me. I know when you talk to her you'll find she's just a poor soul that did it just to grab a few. She's strictly a party broad. I'm sure you can find her right at this moment walking down Seventh Avenue looking for a hot customer."

"Right now," the F.B.I. man answered coldly, "she is not walking around anyplace. She's lying on a slab in the morgue."

"What?" Charlie screamed. "Are you sure it's the same girl? Are you sure it's Sugar? How do you know it's the girl?"

"It's right here on the front page, picture and all. Here—is this the girl?" He handed Charlie the paper.

"Yes, that's her," Charlie said softly. "Poor kid—strangled in her own apartment. It says the maid discovered her body at ten o'clock this morning. The Medical Examiner says she had been dead at least a couple of hours. My God, that means she was killed while those bastards were talking to me. Those dirty Red bastards—those dirty . . ."

"They're thorough," Mr. Simon said, "and they waste no time. They're playing for big stakes and want no witnesses. They take no chances. In case of a tie they kill first and vote later."

"Those dirty crumbs," Charlie spit between his teeth. "I'll get them if it's the last thing I do. I'll—"

"It'll be the last thing you do if you don't do as we tell you. This isn't a TV show. This is for real. Their sponsors are the U.S.S.R. and they will stop at nothing to sell their product—hate. Now, are you ready to work with us and do exactly as we tell you?"

"You're damn right I'm ready," Charlie blared. "Dead Commies are my favorite people. I'll do anything to bury them. Just tell me what to do."

"The first thing you must do is find out what they want you to do. You've got to become one of them," the F.B.I. man said. "Learn everything you can but don't push it. They're masters at propaganda and spying and will notice any false move. One wrong word and you wind up with Candy Sweets. Do you understand?"

"Yes," Charlie answered, "I understand. This could be my last notice, 'Charlie Davis died here!' "

"I'm sure it wouldn't be the first time," the F.B.I. man suggested.

"Et tu, F.B.I.? Everybody wants to get in the act," Charlie answered. "Let's get it straight now. I won't butt into the Federal Bureau of Investigation; don't butt into my racket—I'll tell the jokes."

"That's okay with me," the G man said, "but just remember you're working for the F.B.I. now; you take orders from us."

"Sure," Charlie said. "My next book will be 'I was a comic for the F.B.I.' I think I'll get Cary Grant to play Charlie Davis in the movies—better still, I'll play myself—"

"You'll play dead if you mention one word of this to anybody, even in jest. Talk only to me or somebody from our office who will contact you—nobody else. Most of all, don't be a big hero. Just tell us what you hear or see. What they want you to do. We'll do the rest. Do not do anything on your own. Just do what they tell you to do unless we tell you otherwise. Confide in nobody. And I mean nobody. Not your family or that comic, or anybody. Do you understand?"

"Sure, sure, but how will I know the guy from the F.B.I. if it's not you? How will I contact you? Or whoever?"

"Don't contact us at all. We'll contact you. You'll know our guy when you meet him. You knew me, didn't you? Anyway, he'll mention 'Candy'—and if you say 'that's very sweet of you' and he says 'very funny' you'll know you're among friends."

"But," Charlie protested, "suppose I need you in a hurry."

"Don't worry about that, somebody will be watching you all the time. Every move you make. If you need a fast contact, put a rubber band around your doorknob at home. If you are in the open, like a restaurant, scratch your head with both hands. If you're in the street, stop at the nearest fire hydrant and put your foot up and tie your shoelace—okay?"

Charlie, with his photographic memory, had it all memorized as the man was saying it. This was one script he couldn't afford to fluff. Ordinarily, if he loused up a line the most he could lose was a laugh. Here he could lose his life and he knew it.

"Okay," Charlie agreed and repeated it all back like it was taped.

"And remember," the man warned, "nothing on the telephone or in your apartment or anyplace. You were very smart to have your friend call from a corner booth. Remember, even your car could be bugged. They have it down to a science. They could bug your martini—or the flower in your lapel.

"Those telephone men who worked on this room while you were doing the show were our boys. That's why I can talk to you here—this room is not bugged now. But that doesn't mean that it won't be tomorrow. So, be careful. Just don't talk to anybody unless it's one of us—and then be sure."

"I won't even talk in my sleep," Charlie said. "My wife could be bugged. Which reminds me—is it possible they could really bug anything—I mean anything?"

"That's what I've been trying to tell you."

"Well, I'm worried. I mean suppose I want to—you know—after all, it's my own home. You mean they could be listening?"

"That's right," the F.B.I. man said.

"Well," Charlie said, "let those Red bastards eat their hearts out listening to the master at work and at play."

"You mean," the G man asked, "you are the greatest at that too?"

"Now you're beginning to catch on," Charlie bragged. "I'm just the greatest."

"And modest too."

"I'm tops in humility," Charlie admitted.

Isn't he beautiful? I hope I haven't been giving you the impression that Charlie Davis *likes* himself that much. If I have, I'm sorry. The truth is he *loves* himself that much. Only it's not phony. He really believes he is the greatest. He does do a lot of good for a lot of people. It's just that he lets everybody know about it. Once when I was annoyed that he was running everybody's life, including mine, I blew my top. "Stop playing God," I exploded.

"What do you mean *playing* God?" he gagged. "I *am* God!" Only he wasn't joking.

Now his toughest job wasn't putting his life on the line; it was keeping his name out of the papers. Imagine Charlie Davis working for the F.B.I. and not being able to give the item to the Broadway columnists. On the other hand, if it ever got out that he was working with the Reds, it would kill him.

Nobody wants to be loved as much as Charlie. He answers all his fan mail himself. He'll cross streets or deserts to sign an autograph. Anything to be Mr. Nice Guy. I remember he was offered the top spot in a picture for Joe Levine. It was one of the funniest roles ever given a star. Only the part called for Charlie to play a villain. After reading the script thoroughly, Charlie went to see Mr. Levine. "Look at me," he said to the producer, "look at me. No matter how great an actor I am, do you think I would convince an audience I am not a right guy?" Isn't he beautiful?

Charlie was ready for his role as comic for the F.B.I. He was itching to take on Brezhnev, Kosygin and company and let the Reds fall where they may. He had gone over the whole show in his mind a thousand times and was rehearsed to perfection. But opening night just didn't come.

Each time the phone rang it was like a bomb. Each time he picked it up he figured this was it—only it wasn't. He looked up the nostrils of every stranger that passed, hoping for a word or a sign—nothing. After a week of waiting, he was so nervous, he kept coffee awake.

By the eighth day he was ready to fly to Moscow and grab Brezhnev by his hammer and sickle.

By the ninth day he figured this whole thing was a big fat practical joke planted by me. Now he couldn't rest till he could find me and take me apart—gag by gag. "Imagine," he reasoned with himself, "doing this to the master. And after all I did for him. I'll break that funny bone of his in two and stick it up his nose. I'll run him out of the business. This time it won't be a plant. I'll really do the murder myself . . ."

On the tenth day he awoke with the king of headaches. He knew he couldn't last the day out unless he made some move. He had to know. He got dressed quickly, slipped a rubber band on the doorknob and left the house. When he got to the corner drugstore, he ordered a cup of coffee and cheese Danish. He scratched his head vigorously with both hands before, during, and after his breakfast. When he left the drugstore, he looked for the nearest fire hydrant, stopped, put his leg up, tied his shoelace and then walked to the studio for rehearsal. Now he would know if the whole thing was really on the level or a complete fraud. By the time he reached the TV theater he was feeling much better. It was the waiting that was driving him nuts. Without being able to make a move. Anyway, now he would know . . .

"That man from *TV Guide* is waiting in your dressing room, Mr. Davis," the doorman said. "I hope it's okay. He said you were expecting him."

"Sure," Charlie mumbled. "Sure. Thanks." Pretty quick service, he thought as he bounced up the two flights of stairs without waiting for the elevator.

As he entered the room, Don Simon put his fingers to his lips, pointed to the ceiling, and said, "Hi, Mr. Davis. I hope you don't mind my waiting up here for you—I wanted to take some notes on your dressing room, your clothes, and so on—"

"Sure—sure," Charlie answered. "That's okay. Tell me, when the hell is this damn article coming out? You interviewed me ten days ago and I haven't heard from you or *anybody* since." He put a special accent on anybody.

"It takes time," Simon explained. "You never know when the editor will want to use it. I'm sure he's waiting for the right time. You know, in this business, *timing is everything.*"

"Are you sure they're gonna use it?" Charlie pleaded.

"Are you kidding?" the G man answered. "Do you think they have nothing better to do than play games? They've gone to a lot of trouble to get your story and they're not going to waste it. This is too big a thing to be done slipshod. They got a lot of checking and double-checking to do. And remember all those great pictures they took of you. Cameramen and reporters cost money, you know. Don't you worry, it'll show up sooner or later. Just be a little patient. I'm as anxious for it to appear as you are. Remember, my by-line is on it, too."

"Thanks a lot," Charlie said. "You know what you can do with your by-line if I don't give you the story."

"We'll have to struggle along with people like Bob Hope, Red Skelton, Danny Thomas, Milton—"

"Okay, okay," Charlie interrupted, "I got the finger—you don't have to shove it in."

"I'm only kidding," the man said. "I guess this comedy stuff is catching. Actually, we agree with you that you're the greatest. That's why we're doing a cover story on you."

"I accept your apology," Charlie laughed, "with the greatest animosity. Now what else can I do for you?"

"Actually the story is almost finished. I just wanted to come up here to get some of the color. Maybe I could come to your home one of these days and meet your family. Just to complete the Charlie Davis picture."

"Sure, sure, anything you say," Charlie agreed. "Just tell me when."

"Do you have your scrapbooks at home too?" Don Simon asked.

"Yes."

"Well," he said, "then I can kill two birds with one typewriter. I'll call you tomorrow and set up an appointment."

"Okay," Charlie said, "and thanks for coming up. I'm sorry I blew my top. It's just that I was anxious about it. You know, *TV Guide* is such an important magazine and all."

"I understand," the G man said. As he opened the door to leave, "Just take it easy. The story will be out soon enough. We're not going to waste that beautiful picture we took of you for the cover. Good day—I'll talk to you tomorrow."

On the eleventh day, Charlie did his weekly TV show. He was so busy making with the jokes all day, rehearsing the cast and fighting with his writers, he almost forgot to be nervous. He was too busy thinking about laughs to think about communists and dead bodies and blonde whores and F.B.I. men—almost.

Just like the mailman, neither rain nor storm nor Reds nor corpses could keep Charlie Davis from his audience. He got more laughs than ever, took twice as many falls and wound up with a standing ovation. It wasn't until he got home about four o'clock that morning and started staring at the ceiling that he went back to worrying full time.

He finally fell asleep at about seven in the morning by counting dead Commies. He dreamed about rounding up thousands of Reds single-handed and personally chopping off their heads. At the head of the list was Blondie, Edward G., then Khrushchev, Brezhnev, and Kosygin.

Then he was receiving the Congressional Medal of Honor with LBJ himself presenting it to him before both Houses of Congress and a standing ovation. Now he was kneeling before the Queen as she knighted him Sir Charlie. 'Sir! What will the guys at the Friars say now? They will all have to kiss my ring.'

The cheers were deafening as he rode down Fifth Avenue with LBJ and Mayor Lindsay on either side of him in the biggest ticker-tape parade since Lindbergh. Kids sitting on the shoulders of their parents were hollering, "Sir Charlie— hooray for Sir Charlie."

Everywhere bells were ringing—and ringing and ringing. Suddenly Charlie jumped up. The phone was still ringing. "Yes?" he said sleepily into the speaker.

"This is Ina Borkman," the voice said. "Sugar asked me to call—I have some pictures for you."

An ice-cold shower couldn't wake him faster. "A girl," he shouted into the phone, "you're a girl!"

"I have been for years," she answered. "Any objections?"

"Oh, no, no," he muttered. "Not at all. I just expected— I mean—you know—"

"Well," she interrupted, "man or woman, can you see me now? I'm only across the street and—"

"Sure, sure, come on over. My family are away and we can talk here without being interrupted—just give me five minutes to shower. I'll put on some coffee and—"

"I can hardly wait," she whispered into the phone. "I'm glad we'll be alone," and hung up.

'At least,' he thought to himself as he selected his best robe, 'a bit of femininity will make it nicer.' He dabbed himself with his favorite and most expensive cologne. A girl— how bad could it be: 'Say, this Commie stuff may not be so bad after all.' He smiled to himself.

The bit of femininity that Charlie opened the door for looked like five miles of bad road. "Come in," he said smiling. But his heart wasn't in it.

"I'm sorry to wake you," she said, "but I waited till ten o'clock. I hope I didn't disturb you."

"Not at all," he said with a fixed smile as he gazed at the nightmare in front of him. For a second he thought it was still part of his dream. 'Oh, well, maybe she is a little ugly,' he thought, 'but she sure dresses badly.' She looked like six weeks of stale laundry in her Red Cross shoes, gray blouse and heavy tweed skirt. Now take her face—*please*. Charlie stared at the symphony in garbage in front of him. Her flat nose, milk-bottle glasses, and butch haircut made her look like Khrushchev in *drag*— But the thing that fascinated him was the big black wart with the stiff bristling hairs sticking out of it planted right smack in the center of her chin.

He kept staring at the wart, watching the stiff hairs wavering in the breeze as she talked.

He had a sudden sensation that it couldn't be real. The wart had to be a two-way radio. Those hairs were the antenna and he was sure that she was receiving from a transmitter camouflaged as a mole on the ass of that long-armed ape who had framed him.

"Here's my card," she said as she handed him one of the pictures. It was the one of Charlie and the blonde in bed. "You look like you can make some girl very happy. If you ever decide to go in the business, you can use this picture as an ad."

"Why?" Charlie asked. "Are you interested?"

"Could be," she said coyly. "After all, comrade, we are not made of stone."

'I'd rather go to bed with a stone,' he thought. 'She looks like she fought Sugar Ray for the title—and lost!'

"You know," she said proudly, "communists invented free love."

"It's too good for the Imperialistic Capitalists anyway," Charlie laughed. This was the first time in his life he had ever been alone with a female whom he didn't undress physically or mentally. 'I don't mind giving my all for Uncle Sam,' he thought. 'I regret that I have but one life to give to my country and all that jazz but if I have to make love to this Charles Addams copy I'll become a regular Benedict Arnold. If it's a matter of life and death, Uncle Sam will have to make love to her himself—'

"Now that we understand each other," she said, "how's about getting down to business?"

"You're the boss," Charlie said. "Go ahead—you're on."

"Well," she started, "in the first place, you're on the Ed Sullivan show tonight—right?"

"Right."

"Well, we thought it would help the party if you threw in some jokes against the war in Vietnam and against LBJ—you know, just making fun of them, sort of."

"But Sullivan is very strict about that. He never allows anybody to do any political jokes. Certainly not about the war in Vietnam—he'd never, never let me do it."

"Then why tell him?—Just do it."

"But you don't understand," he explained. "We do a show at one o'clock—sort of a dress rehearsal, with an audience—that's when Ed okays the material for the show at night."

"So," she insisted, "do some different jokes at the dress rehearsal and do these jokes at night."

"Are you kidding?" he said. "He'd hang me. You know what he did to Jackie Mason just for giving him the finger. Ed guards his audience like they were all his children."

"So, it's about time his children learned the facts of life. Anyway," she smiled, "would you rather he hang you or we hang you?"

"Either way I'm dead."

"Aaah—what are you worried about? You don't need Sullivan—you're a big star. You have your own show. And when the revolution comes, he'll be working for you. I'm sure you want to co-operate with us, don't you?"

"Sure," he said, "I want to co-operate—only—oh, okay, I'll figure out some jokes."

"Good! I knew you wouldn't let us down. Now, one more thing. I'd like you to do a show for us at Camp Comrade."

"What the hell is Camp Comrade?" he asked.

"It's a summer resort where our party holds two-week training courses on how to direct civil rights workers and young radicals of the 'new left' into the party. Comrade Gus Hall calls those young people 'the most influential youth organization in this U.S.' "

"What could I do for them?" he asked. "I certainly can't lecture—what the hell do I know about politics?"

"No, no," she said, "I just want you to entertain them. They should see that big stars like you are interested in the movement. We have enough lecturers. Mrs. Helen Winters, wife of Carl Winters, one of the first convicted under the Smith act. James Edward Jackson, publisher of *The Worker*, etc. All we want you to do is amuse them. You know, a little relaxation from the all-day classes. If it's good enough for the Capitalists at Grossingers, it's good enough for our youngsters."

"Okay," Charlie said. "When do we go?"

"Tomorrow!"

"You don't waste time, do you? Okay, but not before twelve noon. Any time after that is fine with me."

"I'll pick you up at 12:01," she said. "It's about seventy-five miles from here—should take us about two hours and I want you to see some of the classes at work before dinner.

It'll do your heart good to see these young students from all over the country speaking up on the role of the working class, Black Power, civil rights and Marxists'-communists' concepts."

"How many will be up there?"

"About two hundred," she answered. "During the summer over two thousand will have taken the course. And they are hand-picked from all over America to carry on the work. Comrade Hall said only last week: 'The fact that youths are coming into the communist party of the United States is a most important distinguishing feature of our time.' "

'The little rats, the dirty little Red rats,' he thought to himself. 'They come from all over our beautiful country to be fed this poison and then they go back to spread the plague and I'm supposed to help them? I'm supposed to entertain them?'

"Okay, comrade," she announced as she patted him on the thigh. ('A little high for a comrade,' he thought, 'but don't argue with a party member.') "I'll look forward to watching you tonight and I'll see you at twelve-one tomorrow." All the time she was patting his thigh.

Charlie jumped up before she started to look good to him. 'Telling anti jokes for my country is one thing. Even entertaining these little Red bastards. But this is going too far. No filthy communist will get *my* body. They don't deserve such pleasure. Especially Comrade Ugg here. I'd have to bathe her in lye and then put a mask over her face.'

Out loud he said, "Okay, Comrade Borkner. I'll be ready. I'll meet you downstairs at twelve-one on the button."

"You can call me Ina," she cooed. She looked like a mongoose in heat.

"Okay, Ina," he said as he walked her to the door. "It's been a pleasure."

"The pleasure," she crooned, "will come later."

'Good God,' he thought as he closed the door, 'I'd rather make it with a snake.'

Charlie Davis was really a smash at the one o'clock show. Bob Precht, Ed Sullivan's producer son-in-law, came to his dressing room and raved about his performance. "Keep it exactly that way tonight. That's the funniest eight minutes we ever had on 'Toast of the Town.' We have to cut three minutes out of this show but we'll have to find it someplace else. Don't change a thing. Ed says he wants you for six more appearances."

"Thanks," Charlie mumbled. "Did he mind the lines I did about him?"

"Mind? He loved them. Especially the one about 'You can sum up Smiley's success in one word—lucky.' And when you said, 'There's a new Ed Sullivan doll on the market. You wind it up and for one hour it does nothing,' I thought Ed would fall off the stage laughing. Don't change a word. He loved the whole thing—exactly as is. After the show tonight, you'll be the talk of the town."

'Yeah,' he thought, 'and I know what they'll be saying.'

"I'll see you later," Bob said. "I have to go and find those three minutes someplace."

"Okay, thanks. See you later," he mumbled.

The phone rang on cue just as the door slammed. "Yes?" he said testily as he picked it up.

"This is Don Simon," the voice said. "I saw the show. Very good."

"Thanks."

"Now, before we put the story to bed, I wanted to check a few facts with you. Have you got a few minutes?"

"Sure—come on over."

"No, I'd rather meet you away from there. You know

—I'd like a few minutes without interruption. How about in front of Lindy's, say in fifteen minutes. We can take a little walk and talk it over—I won't keep you long."

"Fine—I'll be there in fifteen minutes."

The F.B.I. man was waiting for him when Charlie pulled up in the cab. "I hope I haven't kept you waiting too long," he greeted him. And for the people passing by he added, "Those autograph fans—I just couldn't get away."

As they walked down Broadway, "We can talk this way," the G man said, "without worrying about bugs. Just keep it down. Now, I got your message. Oh. Before I forget. Let's drop the rubber-band signal. They might get wise. Especially if I always show up after it. If it's very, very important—just draw your shades down exactly halfway—you have five windows that face Fifth Avenue—right?"

"That's right."

"Okay. Well, draw four halfway and the other all the way and we'll know it's an emergency. Another thing. It's better that I don't meet with you any more. One of the other agents will contact you. Just to keep it on the safe side. After all, how many times do I have to see you for one feature in *TV Guide*?"

"By the way, if they *are* listening and they *are* watching me, what will happen when the story doesn't appear? Won't they think it's funny?"

"It so happens that *TV Guide has* a cover story about you in two weeks."

"How did you do that? I mean, who wrote it? I mean, how did you arrange it?"

"Let's say we have a few connections," he smiled. "Now, what did you want to see me about?"

"They finally made their move. Some Red fink came to see me today—a woman yet, Miss Airedale of 1911. They want me to tell some anti-LBJ and anti-Vietnam jokes on the Ed Sullivan show tonight and they want me to do an act at Camp Comrade tomorrow." Charlie told him the entire story exactly as it had happened, word for word, including the play she made for him. "Okay," he said when he was finished. "What do I do?"

"Why," said the G man, "you go up there and do the show. Just keep your eyes and ears open. Don't ask questions and don't make waves. The most important thing is for you to gain their confidence. Then when they make the wrong move, you'll be in on it and that's when we make *our* move."

"Well, how about those two Red finks that framed me, and the lady monster? Do you just let them run around loose leaving corpses everywhere?"

"That's our job. We have them all under surveillance. If we pick them up too soon it could put you and the whole project in jeopardy."

"Well now, what do I do about the Ed Sullivan show? I can't do any jokes about the war in Vietnam. I can't do any anti-Johnson gags. Doing an act for a bunch of crummy Commies is one thing, but abusing the President of the United States before millions of Americans—"

"Shhh—keep it down," he whispered as he put his hand on Charlie's shoulder, "and don't look so angry. I know how you feel. This is a tough one. You don't have to go too far. Just a few gags to satisfy them—"

"Satisfy them? They won't be satisfied until our whole country is destroyed. Don't you see, I'd be helping them— helping them spread the poison—that's just want they want—"

"I know," he said soothingly. "Propaganda is their biggest weapon. Creating fear and panic. Their only aim is to tear down everything we stand for. And when we take them in custody they are the first to wrap themselves in the red-white-and-blue and holler for their 'rights' under the Constitution—"

"And you want me to help these rats?"

"No—I want you to help trap them. And if holding out a little cheese in the form of a few jokes will do it, I'm all for it. I'm sure you understand that they didn't go to all this bother of framing you just to make you tell a few bad jokes on TV. They must have something important in mind for you and we want to find out what that is—"

"If I live that long. Meanwhile, what do I tell Sullivan?"

"You tell him nothing—*now*. At the right time he'll find out and I'm sure he'll understand."

"Yeah. But what'll I do *now*? You don't know Smiley. You do one little blue gag and he skins you alive. If I do this kind of joke he'll hang me—on camera—"

"If I know you," Simon said, "you'll have a dozen gags ready for the occasion. Mr. Davis, the department has a lot of confidence in you—"

"Don't worry—I never threw a show in my life. It's just that this whole thing has got me walking into walls. My stomach feels like a Mixmaster. If I don't do what they want they expose me as a rapist—murderer—Red lover. If I do do what they want, I'm a traitor. How the hell did I get mixed up in all this?"

They reached 36th Street and Broadway. At four o'clock on Sunday afternoon there wasn't a soul around. It was like the desert with skyscrapers.

"I know how you feel," the G man said as he faced him on the lonely corner. "Believe me, we don't want to get you mixed up in any of this. But right now you are the only pipeline to a situation that has been bothering us for some time. With a little luck and your help we can clear up this whole rat pack at one time."

"Let's get the billing right." Charlie was normal again.

"With *my* help and a little luck *second*. Don't worry, the Kid will be right in there. Tell Mr. Hoover if he needs any help, not to be ashamed—"

"Thanks," the G man smiled. "I'm sure the director will be very happy to hear that. Now I think you better get back to the studio. You must have a lot of things to do before the show."

"Yeah," Charlie said, "I gotta go and prepare my ad libs."

They walked back uptown in silence. At 40th and Broadway Don Simon hailed a cab. "Can I drop you?" he asked.

"No, thanks," Charlie answered, "I think I'll walk. I may have to get used to it after the show tonight."

"If it's any consolation to you, I'll be rooting for you. And remember, even though you don't see me, I'll be around."

"Don't worry about a thing," Charlie said. "When that spotlight hits me, I'm a tiger. I won't need any help. Just get the ambulances ready for the poor souls who will be passing out from laugh cramps."

The F.B.I. man was smiling as he got into the cab. "And good luck with your girl friend tomorrow. I'll keep my fingers crossed."

"Yeah," Charlie answered, "and I'll keep my legs crossed."

Ordinarily, this would have been an easy day for Charlie Davis. After the one o'clock show, especially if Sullivan and Precht approved the routine without any changes, he had nothing to do until make-up at seven o'clock. But now he had to insert some fresh material and in this case it was too fresh.

Charlie is a perfectionist. Even if he was doing this for the F.B.I. *and* Uncle Sam *and* the Commies, the most important thing was the laughs. Don't misunderstand, our hero is a passionate American. He would sacrifice anything for Uncle Sam—anything, that is, but laughs. I think if he had to die for his country he would do it, but you can be sure he would look for a belly laugh on his exit—otherwise he just wouldn't go.

This was a tough one. He couldn't go to his writers. They would never write that kind of gags against LBJ and the war in Vietnam. And he couldn't explain it to them. Also, he had to sneak the lines in before Sullivan could stop him. And most important, they had to be funny.

He walked all the way back to the Ed Sullivan theater on 53rd and Broadway. He was so absorbed in working out the gags, he didn't even notice the line that had formed outside the TV theater. Usually it was a big entrance for Charlie. Now he just passed by without even waving at the screaming kids who recognized him.

I'll tell you how tense he was—he didn't even supervise the make-up man. Like I said, Charlie is a perfectionist. Even if it's not his own show, he likes to tell the director, producer, conductor, press agent, stagehand, and doorman how to do their jobs. Now he just sat there staring into his funny bone as the make-up man took those lumps away from under his eyes, filled in the thinning hair line and plastered on the special goo that the color cameras love.

"Are you okay, Mr. Davis?" the face painter asked.

"Sure, sure," he answered perfunctorily.

"Is the make-up okay?"

"Great—great," he answered, not even looking into the mirror.

"Are you sure you're okay?" the man pressed.

"Okay," Charlie mumbled as he walked out of the room.

He walked down the flight of stairs to his dressing room. He didn't even talk to his manager and press agent, who were sitting there waiting for him. He got into his blue silk mohair and walked the last mile to the stage with his manager and press agent trailing behind in silence.

When Smiley introduced him he suddenly came alive. The spotlight was like a shot in the arm. The first laugh was better than adrenalin. By the third joke he was really rolling.

"What an audience!" he said to them. "You laugh at the questions."

"Did you hear about the two Jewish astronauts? One said 'Forget the moon—we'll go direct to the sun,' and the other said, 'If we go within thirteen million miles of the sun we'll melt,' and the first one said, 'Okay, then we'll go at night.'

"One thing—we'll never have women astronauts. They would never all agree to wear the same style suit.

"An astronaut went into space and back in fifteen minutes. Big deal. I'd like to see him go crosstown in that time.

"I talked to one space jockey who actually took pictures of the moon. He tells me the women up there are built different. They have their chest in the back. It doesn't make them more attractive but it's better for dancing."

As the waves of laughter rolled in Charlie forgot his fears and frustrations about doing the anti jokes. Right now he would stab his grandmother for a class A yock.

"Congress is thinking of asking LBJ to take a trip to the moon—they figure the best way he could serve his country would be by leaving it."

There were enough Republicans to laugh at it—he even got a hand. That's all he needed. Now they came fast and furious.

"Don't misunderstand, I love LBJ. He's tall, dark, and has some fourteen million bucks. When he became President, he put the White House in his wife's name.

"And if he continues the war in Vietnam, there will be a 'For Sale' sign on the White House.

"Who said War is Hell? Not LBJ. What does he care?—he's got two daughters.

"But as LBJ did say, 'I'd rather be right than President.' As it's going now, he won't be either after the next election.

"That torch parade at Fuller University wasn't for the President—it was just the graduating class burning their draft cards.

"But don't worry, Mr. President, I'm with you. You have my vote—but I also voted for Tom Dewey, Alf Landon, and Wendell Willkie, and you know what happened to them. Good night, everybody."

Everybody was screaming but Sullivan. As they met in the center of the ring Charlie put his hand out as always. Ed ignored it as he turned his back on him and started to talk to the audience. If ever he was entitled to be called Stoneface this was it. When the audience kept applauding, Ed just held his hands up for silence. "I don't know what I'd do without him," he borrowed an old Joe E. Lewis line, "but from now on I'm sure going to try." The audience howled, not knowing Smiley was never more serious in his life.

Charlie never stopped to listen to the reaction or Ed's remarks. He walked off stage, into the elevator, down to the ground floor and into a waiting cab before the applause even died down. He didn't even stop to pick up his music, his suit, or a pat on the back from his manager.

Any other Sunday night after a big shot like this Charlie would be all over town taking bows—with his entourage. Dinner at Voisin, a drink or two at Danny's, a stopover at the Stage Delicatessen, and a late visit to El Morocco—but not tonight. He couldn't take the chance of bumping into Sullivan. Right now he couldn't face him, or anybody that would take a rap at him.

Charlie headed for home alone, without food or bows or the morning papers. It was like the bad little boy who is sent to his room without supper—only in this case he was doing it to himself.

Don't misunderstand. Charlie has murdered celebrities before. He has cremated people in the news. At the Ed Sullivan dinner he said, "Everybody says Ed has a dull personality. That's not true. He has no personality at all." At a Friars party he said about Milton Berle, "He hasn't an enemy in the world—but all his friends hate him." About Ike he said, "I'm just like Eisenhower, once I make up my mind I'm full of indecision."

At these roasts, it's the thing to do. You've got to murder the guest of honor or he'll think you hate him. Most comics pay their writers extra to come up with these stiletto lines to stab their best friends in the back. As them theatrical folks say—that's Showbiz.

But this was different. Charlie had worked hard to elect LBJ. He loved him. He felt he had enough troubles without a "friend" taking advantage of the President of the United States just because he had freedom of gags.

'I'm sure the Prez will understand,' he assured himself, 'especially when he finds out I was working for the F.B.I.— I'll be bigger than ever. And did you hear the laughs. I gotta admit I was funny tonight.' All night he dreamed about medals and honors as they were hanging him from the lamppost at Times Square.

The mongoose was waiting for him in her 1954 Edsel when Charlie came down at 12:01. The doorman had called up to say, "There's a person waiting for you downstairs, Mr. Davis. Says she has an appointment with you."

"Does it look like a guerrilla fighter?"

"That might be an apt description, sir."

"Very well, tell it I'll be right down."

"I must kiss you for that show last night, comrade," she greeted Charlie as he slipped into the seat beside her. She grabbed him like he was a bundle of wet wash.

'She's not a guerrilla fighter,' he thought, 'she's a gorilla.'

"Ina," he said when she pulled away from the curb, "you sure know how to kiss." To himself he said, 'She must have trained by blowing up footballs! If this is what I get for a few jokes—what will happen if I'm a big hit on the show tonight?'

"If you're a good boy—I may let you take advantage of me," she answered as she groped for his thigh. 'A little higher,' he thought, 'and she'll hit the jackpot—only this is one machine that is *not* going to pay off. Imagine making love to her and the whole thing being recorded on the wart on her chin.'

"I don't deserve it," he said, looking at her mini skirt with the two fire hydrants sticking out of it. 'She looks more like Mini Mouse.'

"If you do a good show for me tonight," she leered, "I'll do a good one for you."

'For the first time in my life,' he thought, 'I may have to throw a show.' "Tell me," he asked, "why me? I know I'm beautiful and desirable and everything but do I get all these goodies just for telling a few stale jokes?"

"Propaganda," she answered, "is our greatest weapon."

"I know," he said, "but don't tell me the party went to all this bother—murder, sex, frame, blackmail—just to get me to do some gags about LBJ and make funny for the kids at Camp Comrade."

"I have great plans for you," she smiled.

"Yeah. But what do I do when I get out of bed? Don't get me wrong. I ain't knocking it. It's just that I like to know the score."

"You can be invaluable to the party," she explained. "In the first place, you can introduce us to the people that run the talk shows on television and radio—like Joe Pyne—Alan Burke—"

"Are you kidding? That's like tuning in the scene of an accident. They only bring guests on their shows so they can make minced people out of them . . ."

"Meanwhile," she interrupted, "we get our messages across. I have a list here of shows that would be very important for us." She dragged out a yellow sheet of paper from her bosom that Charlie felt sure was glad to get the hell out of there. "Barry Gray—David Susskind—Steve Allison in Los Angeles—the Tonight Show—Merv Griffin—Mike Douglas—Joe Franklin—"

"Look," Charlie tried to explain, "I want to co-operate. But you don't know those guys. Barry Gray eats Commies like you for breakfast. You wouldn't last three minutes on his show. Steve Allison is an old Red fighter from way back. Even when he's driving he wouldn't make a left turn. And as far as David Susskind is concerned, he talks so much you wouldn't be able to get a word in sideways unless you bought time on his show. So what's the use?

"As for the TV shows like Griffin, Douglas, Franklin, and so on, if you tried to say anything serious, they'd laugh you out of the studio or go into a commercial. Either way you don't have a Chinaman's."

"Thanks for the advice," she said solemnly, "but if you don't mind, *we'll* make the decisions. Believe me, we know what we're doing. We have a list of comrades who can take very good care of themselves. All we want you to do is introduce us—we'll do the rest."

"Don't say I didn't warn you."

"Okay," she answered, "we've been warned. Now, one more thing. You're a delegate to three showbusiness unions—AGVA, AFTRA, and Screen Actors Guild. Right?"

"Yop."

"Well, I think it's a disgrace that they make you take a loyalty oath before you can take office. Now they want the members to take the oath before they can carry a card. If that's democracy—then I'm a monkey's uncle—"

'Not a monkey's uncle,' he thought, 'a monkey's aunt.'

"So," he asked, "what do you want me to do about it?"

"I want you to fight against it. It's a product of the fascistic, imperialistic, capitalistic classes. It takes away your civil liberties. It abuses your civil rights. It's anti-American."

"Where do I sign?" he smiled. "I'm with you."

"And I'm with you too," she said as she took his left hand and brought it to her bosom.

"Say," he said, "that Jayne Mansfield had nothing on you." ('I've seen better on cows,' he thought, 'and they give milk besides.')

"You and I can make such beautiful music together," she purred.

'Is she kidding?' he thought. 'She even talks off key.'

"There it is," she said gleefully, "Camp Comrade."

They drove up to what looked like a dirty old outhouse with a wooden gate on either side of it. Tacked on the gate was a bright red sign: "Private Property—No Trespassing."

The skinny youngster who came out of the outhouse to see who was approaching their hallowed grounds couldn't have been more than seventeen. He sported a black beard with nails to match. His T-shirt, shorts, and sneakers were early filth.

"Oh, Comrade Borkman, it's you." He managed a feeble smile. "Welcome to Camp Comrade," he said to both of them, putting his best dirty foot forward as he opened the gate.

The mongoose just nodded and waved with her palm inward like the Queen of England.

The camp is built on the side of a mountain divided in half by a macadam road. On the high side are about twenty-five or thirty bungalows, most of them run-down. Here the help is housed. The main mess hall is also situated there. And a bigger mess you never saw.

It is in the bungalows along the lake-front area that the flower of the American communists—the stinkweeds—are housed. "These youngsters," Charlie's girl friend lectured, "are hand-picked by the party as good prospects to infiltrate America's young in search of new members. These youths come from many sections of the country, some from as far away as San Francisco."

'That guard at the outhouse was certainly a perfect ad,' Charlie thought.

The camp is deep in the forest of New York's Harlem Valley about eighty miles north of New York City. Reminiscent of an old western ghost town, it sprawls across eighty miles of dense woodland on Lake Ellis completely surrounded by trees, foliage, and underbrush.

Camp Comrade was known as Camp Lively in the old days before World War II and accommodated some 800 gay souls looking for fun, romance, or a rich husband. Today no more than 200 could be accommodated and the only fun in the whole joint is getting the hell out of there.

Most of the seventy or eighty bungalows have seen years of abuse. Some are reduced to lean-tos. The softball field, basketball, tennis, and handball courts are all overgrown with weeds.

"Our youth are too serious," the mongoose explained, "to be bothered with these silly imperialistic games."

"How about something to eat?" Charlie suggested. "Or is that strictly a capitalist luxury?"

They both laughed. "We're just in time," she said, "it's two-fifteen. Everybody breaks for lunch at two and classes don't start again until three-thirty—so you've got plenty of time to feed your soul."

"Hey, that's very good." Charlie patted her on the back. "You're a regular Edna St. Vincent what's-her-name."

"I think I better feed you before you get delirious. You're a growing boy and you'll need the strength," she drooled as she massaged his thigh.

'Strength?' he thought. 'Strength? What I'll need is guts if she expects me to give her my all for the party.'

The dining sty was a large open gazebo with about twenty tables and ten little pigs at each table ranging in age from seventeen to twenty-five. Dressed in T-shirts and shorts, most of the kids looked hardly old enough to shave, although some of the girls could have used a nice sharp Gillette.

There were about four boys to each girl and every table had at least one or two Negroes and Spanish-speaking youths.

Food was put in the center of the table—country style. It smelled like it came from the old country. Each person helped himself. Charlie was lucky enough to sit down at a table near the door, next to a young radical with the biggest mustache in the camp—and it was a girl. She had the personality of a social disease and was just as annoying.

"I think it's a product of fascistic dictatorship," she was screeching when Charlie and the warden sat down. Her voice was so high only dogs could hear her. "I'm against all prayers in schools," she squealed. "It's a capitalistic plot to make the masses bow under the yoke of imperialism—don't you agree, comrade?" She aimed this last at Charlie.

"I don't even understand the question," Charlie smiled.

"We were talking," she squeaked, "about God in the classroom—"

"Well," Charlie cleared his throat, "I don't see where it could do any harm. I mean, if you believe in God—"

"Oh, come on." She looked at him like she was an Arab and she knew what he was. "You don't believe in that crap, do you?"

"Well," he said, "all I can tell you is that there are more churches and synagogues in America than ever before—"

"So what?" she squawked. "In the U.S.S.R. they have over forty churches but only the old and the illiterate attend."

"Forty churches in all of Russia?" Charlie laughed. "There were more churches on my block in Brooklyn." The mongoose kicked him under the table.

"This is not a laughing matter," the young anteater shrilled. "These are serious times. If the proletariat doesn't stand shoulder to shoulder . . ."

But Charlie had tuned her out by now. He was watching a pretty little girl at the end of the table. In her clean white blouse, her red hair piled neatly on top of her head, and little gold loop earrings, she stood out in the crowd like a rose in a condemned building.

Charlie noticed that she didn't seem to be part of the revolution going on around her. She neither cheered nor deplored the ugly little radical who was piercing the air with her shrieks. She just sat there sadly with her big blue eyes focused on Charlie—like she needed a friend.

"Comrades," Ina Borkman called out, "I thought you'd like to meet my guest—his name is Charlie Davis." It was like she said Sam Schnitzer. The reaction was a resounding silence. "He's the biggest star on television," she pressed on. "You should have heard him last night on the Ed Sullivan show. Did he give it to LBJ!"

"I don't have a television set," the little fat boy with the horn-rimmed glasses spoke up. "It interferes with my reading."

"Neither do I," echoed the anteater. "It's a product of the capitalistic class to force their imperialistic propaganda on the unsuspecting masses."

"I wouldn't have a set in my house," the long kid with the pimples chimed in. "It's a time waster. There are too

many serious problems facing the world—the Negro question
—American aggression in Vietnam . . ."

"If I depended on you," Charlie laughed, "I'd still be
toomling on the Borscht Belt."

"Mr. Davis has consented to do a show for us tonight,"
the guerrilla interrupted. "Right after dinner in the central
meeting hall."

This exciting news was greeted with another outburst of
silence. "Thanks for the round of indifference," Charlie
gagged, "and up yours too." 'Now if I could just kick that
little fat bastard in his red square—' he thought as he got up
to leave. On his way out he patted Fatso on the belly. "Listen
to me," he cracked, "have it lanced."

Ina put her arm in Charlie's as they walked down the
dining-room steps. "Don't feel badly," she tried to console
him. "These are serious-minded youngsters. Most of them
are members of the DuBois clubs and they want to learn as
much as they can in this two-week indoctrination course to
take back to their organizations back home. Their only
thoughts are concerned with the role of the working class,
civil rights, the concepts of Marx, Lenin, and the like—they
have no time for fripperies."

"Then why did you bring me up here?"

"Because I think they need a little relaxation. And after
dinner, when all the classes and lectures are over, they'll be
ready for it. I'm sure they'll love you—especially if you do
those LBJ jokes—and anyway, it will do you a lot of good
to see what the Youth of America really is thinking."

'The flower of American Youth,' he thought, 'blooming
idiots.' Out loud he said, "Anything you say, Master, I'm with
you."

"And I'm with you too," she giggled, patting him on the
derriere—his thigh wasn't available. "I've got some business
to do but don't go away. Just make yourself at home—you

can visit any of the classes you like. The place is yours. I'll catch up with you later," she said as she gave him a parting grab on the fanny.

The classes were divided into groups of twenty to thirty, each stirring up its own brand of poison. "We must bring about a radical change in the United States," one bald-headed lecturer was telling his charges, "and put an end to this country's aggressive foreign policy."

It was a particularly hot day and all the classes were out in the open. As Charlie walked along the water front he could feel the hostility filling the air. One middle-aged lady in charge of venom for her group was asking "whether it is better to work with one ethnic group to foster upheavals or to gain the confidence of several minority groups."

One grimy little slob with the personality of a shoe box gave an inaudible answer and then sat down to thunderous applause from the class. A young girl who looked like sixteen then gave her important opinion.

Charlie sat down on the grass in front of the main building where the biggest class was forming on the porch. About forty little Reds were hanging around listening to some bore holler about "infiltrating civil rights meetings—CORE, NAACP, SNIC. We must get them to join the party . . ."

'At least,' Charlie thought, 'it shouldn't be a total loss. I'll get a little sunshine.'

"I beg your pardon." It was the redhead with the sad eyes. "Could you please give me your autograph, Mr. Davis? I'm a fan of yours."

"Sure, sweetie," he smiled, "you just saved my day. Here," he said patting the grass, "sit down next to me."

"Oh, thank you," she said sweetly.

"Say," he grinned, "without that table in front of you, you really sport a gorgeous hunk of body. You make these other broads look like boys."

"Thank you," she said without listening. "Mr. Davis, I must talk with you. I need your help. I'm in terrible trouble. I hope I'm doing the right thing—but I must take the chance." It all rushed out like Niagara. She grabbed his arm. Her nails dug into his flesh. "Please," she cried, "please help me. They want to kill us—"

"What the hell is this, Candid Camera?" he asked. "Where do you keep the bug—in your navel?"

"Mr. Davis," she pleaded, "I'm desperate—I—"

"Look, sister," he interrupted, "I can smell a phony at twenty paces. Let's get this straight. I'm a good party member. You wanna come to my cell, I'll show you my 8 × 10 blow-up of Trotsky in tights."

"You don't understand," she cried. "You must listen to me. You're my only hope. When I saw you at lunch I knew you weren't one of them. I mean the way you looked disgusted at those kids. Your attitude and all. That's why I came looking for you. Really, I've always been a fan of yours—"

"I know, I'm irresistible," he gagged. "Look. If you're putting me on, you'll wind up in Commie Hell or wherever it is they send bad little Reds. Here! Give me that paper and pencil—what did you say your name was? Marcee De Maye? Good. I'll sign this to Marcee with love and kixxx from Charlie Davis. Now if you must tell me your life story, do it quietly and for God's sake smile. If anybody's watching, you'll ruin my image—I'm supposed to be a comic, you know."

"Oh, thank you," she said, forcing a thin smile, "I feel better already."

"Oh, well," he said, "what have I got to lose. It's gotta be funnier than those vomiters up there. If you're a phony, at least you're a cute one—okay—you're on."

"My father," she started, "has been a big shot in the communist party as long as I can remember. My brother and

I were brought up in it. Although I personally was never really active. You know, sort of a fellow traveler.

"Father is a photographer by profession. About twenty years ago the party helped get him out of Czechoslovakia. He brought my brother and me with him. My mother who was pregnant with my sister remained there, as a hostage. Of course, they didn't admit that. They promised that they would get them out as soon as we got settled here. That's over twenty years ago and they're still there.

"Meanwhile, my father prospered as a photographer. Besides his business, he was the official keeper of the records for the party. It was Father who made all the microfilm for the spy work. It was Father who kept the files on all the party members to make sure they followed orders."

'So that's the bum who has my pictures,' Charlie thought.

"Nothing is left to chance. They have something on everybody. It's Father's job to keep it all on film. They even bought him the house we live in—a brownstone on East 35th Street—that's where all the files are kept. They have one secret room that only my father and two other party leaders know about that is filled with enough material to send almost every big-shot communist in America to the chair.

"I don't need to tell you that Father never stopped trying to bring my mother and sister over here. He even tried to go over there, but he was told he'd never be able to get out again. He did the next best thing. He sent my mom and sister monthly checks.

"Two months ago, after school closed, I went to Russia on a vacation. That's when I really became disillusioned with the communist party. I never saw such fear and poverty in my life. Even if they have money—there's nothing for them to buy. And they want us to change—for *that?*

"Believe me, that girl at the table was so right. Only the old and the illiterate go to church or synagogue in Russia.

Sure. That's because Saturday and Sunday are working days.
Monday is the day off. And if you don't show up for work you
better have a good excuse, like a broken leg—or they'll break
it for you—or they'll take you off the list for an apartment or
send you to Siberia—"

Charlie looked around to see if anybody was watching
or listening. They were all too busy making their own little
pile.

"Anyway," she continued, "when I got my visa for Russia, I also got one for Czechoslovakia. I didn't even tell my
father about it. I had to see my mother and sister—no matter
what.

"Well, to make a long story short and ugly, I found that
my mother had been dead for eight years. They never told us.
Some 'loyal' party member was forging letters from my
mother and keeping the money my father was sending. My
poor little sister never saw a penny of it. She was so poor and
sick she finally turned to streetwalking when she was fifteen
years old—so she could eat—"

Marcee stopped to catch her emotions. Tears were well-
ing up in her eyes and her voice was crying to be patted.

"They're beautiful all right," Charlie said. "And I
thought my agent was bad. Look, sweetie, if anybody sees
you crying I'll lose my reputation as a lover and a funny man.
Although some say my loving is pretty funny at that."

"Thank you," she said, trying to find a smile. "I'm sorry.
It won't happen again."

"Did you hear about the big robbery in Russia?" Charlie
gagged. "Someone broke into the Kremlin and stole next
year's election results."

Marcee actually laughed.

"Say," he said, "for a minute I thought I'd lost the Davis
touch. You know I would never be a hit in Russia. Over there
you don't watch television. Television watches you. I'll tell

you one thing. Russia surprised me. I was treated like a Czar when I was there. And you know how they treated the Czar."

"Gee, Mr. Davis," she laughed, "you're wonderful."

"I admire your taste," he gagged. "Okay. Now finish your story. And no hysterics—please—and remember, you're talking to the No. 1 comedian in the world—except Russia and Camp Comrade."

"I'll remember," she said. "Well, I told you that I found out about my mother and sister. When I came back to the States and told the story to my father and brother, they went berserk. Brother went looking for the rats that were responsible and came back dead. They killed him . . . ."

"Easy now," Charlie reminded. "Now, *who* killed him?"

"Two goons called Roy Darvis and Dirk Jones," she answered. "They're the ones that do all the dirty work for the party."

"Is one a blond and the other dark and short with long arms like a gorilla?"

"Yes," she said, surprised. "How do you know?"

"Never mind," he answered. "Go ahead—how do you know they did it?"

"Because they are the hatchet men. And it's typical of their work. Father has many other examples of their handiwork on file. No doubt about it. Darvis and Jones did it."

"Okay," he said, "go ahead."

"Father went crazy. He threatened to expose the whole party—and everybody in it. He told them he had complete files outside of the house, and if anything happened to me or him they would automatically be turned over to the police."

"Is that true—does he have such files?"

"I have them now. That's why I've come to you. I want you to keep them for us. If they find them on me, my father and I are as good as dead."

"What are you trying to do, make it a trio? Look, sweetie, I'm too young and handsome to die."

"But, Mr. Davis, nobody is safe from them. Sooner or later everybody falls under their ax unless we do something about it."

"We? What do you mean *we*? How do I fit into this? Why me?"

"Because you're in the files too. That body in your car was my brother. That blonde that you took those pictures with was killed by the same two goons—Darvis and Jones. I didn't want to tell you. I didn't want to embarrass you, but you might as well know it all now—I've told you everything else."

"Okay," he said, "I guess I'm it. Where have you got it stashed?"

"Right here," she answered. "It's in my hair piece on top of my head."

"I think you've flipped your lid."

"No, you don't understand," she explained. "It's a roll of microfilm. I got it buried underneath the webbing of my hair piece."

"Well, I'll be a dirty communist," he mumbled. "You mean you got all their files in a little roll of film?"

"There's enough in that little roll of film," she said, "to blow the whole party and everybody in it high, wide, and ugly, like they are."

"Okay," he said. "Now how are you going to get it to me without getting scalped?"

"Easy," she said, scratching her head and palming the atomic film, "shake." Charlie shook her hand and became the new custodian of the hottest piece of film since Marilyn Monroe.

"Well," Charlie said, "I think we better break this up before somebody digs the scene. If they don't have the grass bugged we may be in the clear." He got up and then helped Marcee to her feet.

Somebody on the porch was yelling about Black Power.

Charlie didn't wait to hear if he was for or against it. All the classes were still B.S.ing about "the proletariat and the role of the working man." As they walked along the lake front, the same ugly sounds kept reaching them: "Strike," "Pickets," "Lenin," "Marx," "Revolt." Just enough to make you want to throw up.

"You know," Charlie said, "if they weren't so dangerous they'd be laughable. Every time one of those punks shoots off his mouth I keep thinking of Willie Howard's famous soapbox scene: 'Revolt—we are starving while the bosses are eating strawberries and sour cream. Comes the revolution, we'll *all* eat strawberries and sour cream. Revolt—those dirty politicians have been robbing you for years—now give *us* a chance.' "

"Believe me," she said, "when you see these files, you'll find very little to laugh about."

"I know," he answered, "but sometimes it's better to laugh than vomit. Anyway, if I don't get to town and get rid of this bomb, they'll cut my laughs out for good."

"Get rid of it?" she quizzed. "What do you mean?"

"Well," he explained, "I don't want to carry it on me. Especially with that Ina Borkman around. She's got more hands than a centipede. So far she's touched me everyplace but my imagination. I'm going to try to get to Newburgh and mail it to myself in New York."

"Please be careful," she warned. "They've got their spies everywhere."

"Don't worry," he gagged, "with oiy oiy 7 on the job— nothing can go wrong."

"Thank you for everything," she said. "You're wonder-ful."

"You got good taste," Charlie laughed. "I'll see you at dinner. Is there anything I can get you in town?"

"No, thank you. But you can call my father if it's not

too much bother. I don't even know if he's alive or what. Just tell him I'm okay. I know he must be so worried—I've been here almost a week and I haven't heard a word."

"I don't get it. Doesn't he write to you? I mean, don't you talk to him on the phone?"

"No student, while undergoing training, may receive phone calls or mail addressed to the camp. Letters must be addressed to a secret mail drop in Brooklyn and from there delivered by courier to the camp. So far I haven't heard a word."

"Well," he said, "welcome to Camp Comrade Concentration Camp." He took her phone number and promised to call and report to her when he came back. "If I can get out of here—"

Charlie found Ina Borkman in the office of the main building. That is, the girl at the office called her and put her on the phone with him. "I'd like to borrow your car," he said casually. "I have to go to town. I need a shave if you want me to look pretty tonight and I need some Gelusil and a few other things."

"I'll be glad to send one of the boys for whatever you want."

"Will you send my head with it? It doesn't screw off, you know, in spite of what you may have heard."

"Some day," she said, "I may screw it off for you."

"And how do you mean that?"

"Never mind," she laughed. "I don't know what to do with you. I mean, I know what to do with you—but we can't do it over the phone. Where are you—in the office? I'll be right over with the keys."

"Right over" meant about twenty minutes. Of course, she could have sent the keys by messenger but then she couldn't play "Grab Bag" with her new Red ward. She warned him as she walked him to the car, which was still parked in front of the mess hall, to remember that he was not to divulge anything he saw or heard, and to talk to nobody about anything. She punctuated each warning with a fast grab of his behind.

"Thank you," he smiled as he turned the car around. "It's not definite, but you may win the Davis cup yet." He drove past the outhouse and out onto the highway.

The sign was plainly marked "Newburgh 19 miles." 'Say,' he said to himself, 'this is easy. And Don warned me not to take these Reds for granted. They're smarter than you think, he said. They're champs in propaganda and spying, he said. Hey, maybe it's too easy.

'No wonder she kept me waiting twenty minutes before she gave me the keys for the car. She wanted to set up a tail. Naaah. It couldn't be. She just needed the time to set her face and put her bust up in curls. Is it possible she saw me talking to Marcee—or one of her spies did? But if Marcee is on their drop-dead list would they let her talk to me this long? Is it possible they saw her pass me the microfilm? If they did, they'd never let me out of there alive. Maybe they want to see where I go with it. Maybe she did put a shadow on me. Aaaah, what kinda shadow? Soon I'll be looking for Lamont Cranston. . . .'

Charlie was scared. It was the first time in his life he had ever been nervous. As he drove along he kept looking around to see if he was being followed. He felt something ominous was about to happen.

'What the hell am I so nervous about?' he thought. 'I wasn't nervous in Saigon when I was doing shows for the boys while they were dropping bombs around me. The only thing is, if they cut my throat, how will I tell the jokes? What am I talking about? Why should I be nervous? When you gotta go you gotta go. Anyway, who's afraid to die? Remember the time I died in Scranton? I survived, didn't I? And look where

I am today! Where am I? I'm in big trouble if they catch me with this goddam film. . . . All I gotta do is put it in an envelope, mail it to myself, and I'm the biggest hero of the year. On the other hand . . .'

The conflict was still going on inside him when he drove into Newburgh, a nervous wreck. He looked for the center of town and deposited the Mixmaster he was driving in front of the Newburgh Hotel. "Shall I park it?" the doorman asked.

"No," Charlie quipped, "preserve it." What did I tell you? All he needs is an audience of one and he's back to his old lovable self again. "Do you want a good tip?" he asked the doorman.

"Sure," the man said.

"Well, don't drive the car—it's liable to explode."

'Good boy!' Charlie said to himself. 'Just do what you always do—only this time tip the man; you'll need all the friends you can get. And act natural. You always say you're the greatest actor in the world. Okay, now's the time to prove it.'

Charlie walked into the hotel like he didn't have a care in the world or an atomic film in his pocket. He played the lobby like the big TV star. Signed autographs, threw his quips at the bellhop who directed him to the barbershop. After a little organized confusion and a shave, Charlie lent his august presence to the drugstore, where he invested in a small box of Gelusil and a tin of aspirin.

By now he had taken over the whole hotel. People came out of the woodwork to see the big celebrity from New York. Charlie was enjoying it so much he almost forgot his mission. Almost. "Say," he said to his bellhop pal, "where can I get some stationery and stamps?"

"The stationery is on the desk in the corner," he said pointing, "and the stamps you can get from the stamp machine at the newsstand—do you want me to get them for you?"

"No, thanks. I like to play the slot machines myself." Charlie was used to eyes watching him wherever he went and he never let them down. Now he had to play it bigger and broader than ever in case the wrong eyes were looking.

He put a quarter in the machine and pocketed the stamps that he won. "I promised to send a little note to the President," he quipped to the lady behind the counter. "He wants my advice on what to do about the gas bill—I'm gonna tell him to pay it."

He strutted over to the writing table, sat down with his back toward the dozens of eyes that were watching his every gesture, and scribbled away, whistling all the time. When he was finished, he nonchalantly put his hand in his right pants pocket where he had stashed the stamps and made a big gesture of licking the stamps and the envelope and banging down with a resounding wallop to seal it.

"Hey, lieutenant," he said to the bellhop, "where's Uncle Sam's box? Where do I mail my advice to the lovelorn?"

"At the elevators," he answered. "Can I drop it for you?"

"No thanks," Charlie gagged, "if you drop it, it'll break."

He took the long walk to the other side of the lobby, answering greetings as he went along. People coming out of the elevator did a double-take when they saw the familiar TV face come alive.

'Another second,' he thought, 'and it's all over.' He held the flap of the mailbox open with his left hand and held up the envelope with his right to deposit it.

A strong hand gripped his wrist and another snatched the letter from his fingers. "I'll mail it for you," the voice said. The man behind the hands was about six feet tall and just as wide in the shoulders.

"Hey," Charlie blurted out, "what the hell are you doing? That's my letter."

"Don't worry, we're just watching it for you," the man said softly, but to Charlie it came out like thunder. "Comrade Borkman asked us to watch out for you—so—we're watching."

"Look, pal," Charlie finally caught his breath, "you can get twenty years tampering with the U.S. mail. All I have to do is give one yell and you're a dead pigeon—"

"Go ahead," the man warned. "One yell and you're a dead Jew. There's a man behind you that would just love to blow your head off. He hates comedians—especially loud ones."

"You'll be sorry for this," Charlie bluffed. "I'll have Miss Borkman cut your heart out—"

"Look, comrade," said the man sarcastically, "I have no heart. Now, will you stop making like an actor and let me read this letter. I love short stories. Who's Arthur Davis?"

"That's my son," Charlie answered.

"You certainly must like the kid. I mean, to come all the way into Newburgh to write him a letter. Say, this is the fattest letter I ever saw. What have you got in it—diamonds?"

"If you must stick your fat nose in my business, it's money. I forgot to send him his weekly allowance at camp. Now, will you please give me back my letter. This is personal. It has nothing to do with you or Borkman or anybody."

"Sure, after I see what's inside. Can I help it if I'm inquisitive?" He tore open the envelope. "Say," he said stupidly, "you really *do* have money in here. This *is* a letter to your son."

"Well, what the hell do you think I've been trying to tell you?" Charlie answered as he grabbed the money and the letter out of the man's hand.

"So," said the man coldly, "I made a mistake. So what do you want me to do—kill myself?"

"That *would* be a nice gesture," Charlie answered. "But first get me a stamp—that's the least you can do."

"Okay," the ape said, "then we'll be even."

"And make it airmail," Charlie called after him.

Charlie walked back to the desk to write the letter to his son again. This time he only addressed one envelope. Before, he had addressed one to himself and one to his son. When he put his hand in his pocket the first time to pull out the stamps, he also extracted his money and the film. He inserted the money in the envelope to his son and the film in the other.

It was easy putting both envelopes together with the flaps up—one slightly lower than the other, licking them together like one envelope, putting the stamps on both letters and sealing them at the same time. With his back toward the lobby and any prying eyes, it looked like only one letter was being worked on.

Meanwhile, it was very simple to slip the other letter into the inside pocket of his jacket where it now rested—stamped, sealed, and ready for the trip to New York.

"Here," the big ape threw at him, "here's the stamp— stick it on your letter."

"Thanks," Charlie answered, "you're sweet."

Charlie stamped the new letter and put it in his inside pocket beside the other one. He took the same long walk to the elevators. When he got there he opened the flap of the mailbox with his left hand like he did before. With his right hand he reached into his breast pocket and pulled out the two letters as one and—deposited them both.

'Whew! I feel like I've gone twenty rounds with Joe Louis and twenty rounds of drinks with his illegitimate son Joe E. . . . Now all I have to do is make the phone call to Marcee's father and then I can rush back to the arms of my beautiful little gorilla who is waiting to grab my behind. I don't care what anybody says about her—they're right.'

The ape man was sitting in an easy chair in the center of the lobby reading a paper but one eye stayed on Charlie. Charlie walked over to him and tapped him on the shoulder. "I've got to make a couple of phone calls," he said sweetly. "I'd invite you in to listen but you could never make that phone booth. But I'll be glad to get you a transcription of my conversation."

The man kept staring at his paper. "After that," he continued, "I'm going back to camp. In fact, you can ride back with me—why use up extra gas following me? Save the party money. Any questions?"

The Mixmaster was sitting in front of the hotel just where he had left it. It wasn't exactly sitting—it was leaning. Charlie didn't dally in front of the car like he does with his Rolls. He got the keys from the doorman, tipped him, and got the hell out of there as fast as the antique could take him.

"Thanks for the goons," he said to the gooness as he threw the car keys on her bed. She had asked him to deliver them to her bungalow.

"I just heard the story," she said contritely. "I'm sorry."

"Sorry? This ape you sent after me has the personality of the inside of a fountain pen. Why should I be followed and humiliated like that? Haven't I done everything you asked me to do? Do you know those jokes I did on the Sullivan show could cost me my career? I talked to my press agent on the phone and he tells me the newspapers killed me today. One columnist even called me a Pinko—and you send King Kong after me?"

"I'm sorry," she said. "This is SOP for the party. We all get checked every once in a while. It's good for us—it keeps us in line. I'm sorry it embarrassed you, really I am, but if I didn't do it I could have gotten in trouble myself. You see, my kids reported to me that you were talking to Marcee De Maye for a long time. It happens that we are concerned about her. She may have something that belongs to the party. Now if she gave it to you, it could cause a lot of trouble. This way, you are free and clear—"

"She just seemed like a nice kid," he explained. "She asked me for my autograph—that makes her a smart kid. She was telling me about her father and how he is the only one she has left. When I told her I was going to town she asked me to call him and tell him she's okay. She said students can't receive or send any mail, or use the phone, and she was sure he was worried about her. Now what's wrong with that?"

"Nothing," she said. "Did you call her father?"

"Of course," he answered. "The man was so grateful I thought he'd crawl through the phone and kiss me."

"Did he know who he was talking to?"

"Naturally. It cost me sixty cents to make the call— why shouldn't I get the billing?"

"I'm glad you told me all this on your own," she said quietly. "You see, Mr. De Maye's phone is tapped. He has been causing us a little anxiety lately. I got a phone call a few minutes after you talked to him. This gives you a clean bill of health. I'm glad. You could mean so much to the party— and *me*." She accented the last by grabbing a handful of the Davis anatomy.

"If I mean so much to you," he said, pulling away, "how come you're still checking on me? When do I graduate?"

"Right now!" she said as she turned off the light. "I'm going to give you your diploma right now!"

Dear Reader, you can beat me, shoot me, stab me, hang me, this is as far as I can go with this incident in the life of Charlie Davis. God knows I've tried to be authentic throughout this narrative. I've spent hour after hour, day after day, in the early morning hours when he couldn't sleep and the

late afternoon when he was fresh and ready to talk, just to
get every little detail of this story correct—including his in-
ner thoughts and his outer ham. I've got him recorded down
to his last belch.

But I just couldn't get him to talk about what happened
when the lights went out. It's a complete blackout. I tried
everything from man-to-man talks to large doses of sodium
pentathal. Nothing.

As near as I can make of it, he just closed his eyes, held
his nose and jumped.

I can't understand it. Charlie is always the first to talk
about his sex appeal. He has told me in intimate detail about
his exploits with Lana, Ava, and Liz. Of course, I mean Lana
Wortmann, Ava Traum, and Liz Heller.

What I *can* tell you is that when he left the gorilla's
bungalow he was a broken and beaten man. I do know he
pranced into her cage at exactly 5:36 a gay, happy, and
healthy man—and crawled out at 7:02 a dead Jew.

Anyway, I hope you'll forgive this short lapse in the
thrilling saga of Charlie Davis. If you had any class, I'm sure
you'd be the first to deny it if you were ever attacked by a
man-eating gorilla.

At any rate, there's nothing I can do about it. I'll just
have to pick up the story from the moment he left her bungalow—panting.

Dinner revived our hero somewhat. It wasn't the food.
The stuff they were serving could kill more communists than
J. Edgar Hoover. It's just that he was finally able to get a little
air. After a couple of drinks his batteries were recharged
enough to do the show.

Charlie sat next to Marcee at dinner. Comrade Borkman never showed. Like any beast of the jungle, after a full
meal she curled up and went to sleep.

Of course, Marcee was anxious about her father. "He

was so glad I called. I told him you were in good shape—and I mean just that."

"Thank you—thank you," she said. "How did he sound? Is he okay?"

"Oh, he sounded like he knew he was talking to the whole network. But he's fine. He recognized my voice and was coldly pleasant—sends his love."

"How can I ever thank you?" she asked lovingly.

"Oh, there are ways," he answered with a gleam in his eye. But right now that's the only place he had a gleam. He was just storing it up for a cold winter.

Charlie told me he was a big hit in the second show. That is, the one on stage. I have checked and double-checked every part of this story. Now, I don't know any communists. And if I did I certainly wouldn't be interested in their opinion of Charlie Davis' comedy. So, he was a big hit. What have we got to lose if we take his word for it? It doesn't interfere with the authenticity of the rest of the story. I only know that Ina Borkman was pleased. She came out to see the show and drove him back to New York without grabbing him once—there was nothing left to grab.

From out of the fog that surrounded the Davis epic, following the attack of the monster lady, one thing comes out sharp and clear. Charlie was in. That doesn't mean they weren't going to check him or bug him twenty-four hours a day. In the Red society, nobody's status is permanent, as Comrade Khrushchev will tell you—if they ever let him open his mouth again.

Anyway, on the way home, Ina showed him where he stood with the party. She had shown him everything else. Now she asked him to spy on Comrade De Maye. "Get friendly with the girl—she seems to have a crush on you. Win her confidence—go to her home. With your personality you could win the devil himself."

"Thanks, but after I win his confidence—what?"

"Well, Comrade De Maye has been a very faithful and valuable worker in the party for as long as I can remember. For many years he has kept all the party records. Recently he had a bad blow. His wife died in Czechoslovakia and his son was killed here in an accident. He blames us. Of course there is no foundation to that, but you can't reason with a hysterical man.

"He told us he has made microfilm of all the records and has it in a safe place outside his home. By the way, your record and pictures are in that file. He has threatened to expose the whole party and everybody in it if anybody touches him or his daughter.

"Naturally, we don't want to hurt him or his daughter. We need him. He was very valuable to us. He still is. But if this film winds up in the wrong hands, it could be a death blow to everything we have worked for, including Comrade De Maye and his daughter—*and* Charlie Davis."

"Well, what can I do about it?"

"You can find out where he keeps it. Tell him you will hold it for him and protect him. You know," she said, chucking him under the chin, "give him the Davis charm. Nobody can resist it."

'Wow. Now I'm counter—counter—counter—counter-intelligence,' he thought. 'First I'm framed to work for the Commies, then the FBI has me working for them while I work for the Commies, now I spy for the Commies against a Commie while working for the FBI. Are you sure Sean Connery started this way?'

As soon as he got home, he pulled the four shades halfway down and the fifth one all the way, thinking 'Now when Don Simon asks "What's new?" boy, will I have something to tell him!'

It was a little after midnight and Charlie didn't expect anybody would see the signal until the morning. It was a pretty early hour for him to go to bed. You can get barred from the Stage Delicatessen for such treachery. But he was really beat. He hadn't slept for days—and the sneak attack hadn't helped either.

Charlie would still be sleeping if that damn bell hadn't gone off. He stuck his hand out of the sheets, pulled the receiver off the hook and took it to bed with him. The ringing continued. He finally crawled out of bed, threw some water on his face and went to answer the door. There was nobody there, but the ringing continued. He stumbled into the kitchen and took the receiver off the house phone.

"There's a special delivery letter. Man says it's registered and you must sign for it. He's been ringing your bell for twenty minutes. Sorry to bother you, Mr. Davis, but your maid isn't here. The letter carrier says it's important."

"Okay—send him up," he said groggily. "What time is it?"

"Nine o'clock."

"Nine o'clock in the morning? Are you crazy? This is sabotage!"

"I'm sorry to bother you, Mr. Davis, but the man says—"

"All right, send him up. Nine A.M.?—you can die from this."

The handsome young Negro letter carrier offered Charlie a yellow slip of paper and the stub of a pencil. "Sign here, Mr. Davis." He set the paper on an open leather case.

After he signed it, the man removed the slip of paper and Charlie saw the card with the legend, "Federal Bureau of Investigation." His picture was there and his name: Bert Rackback. "We got your message," he said.

"What are you doing in a letter carrier's uniform?" Charlie asked.

"We work for the same uncle," he smiled. "Mr. Simon would like to meet you later. Can I help you in the interim?"

"No, thanks. Where do I meet him?"

"It's all there. And please don't take any chances—just do exactly as he says in the letter. Good to meet you, Mr. Davis—and good luck."

Charlie ripped open the letter as soon as the door was closed. "Meet me at 5 P.M. at Teddy's on West Broadway—and please don't come direct. Get rid of any tail. Make sure nobody is following you—and rip this up and flush it down the toilet." It was signed with the initials D.S.

Charlie called the garage from the house phone and asked for his chauffeur.

"He's washing the car," the man said.

"Well, dry him off and send him up to me, will you?"

"Sure, Mr. Davis."

"What are you doing up so early?" the chauffeur asked. "You can be thrown out of the actors' union for this. You're up before the Rolls."

"Goldfarb, the one thing I do *not* need now is a chauffeur who tells jokes. Especially at nine o'clock in the morning, when I can't think of a topper."

"I'm sorry, Mr. Davis, but being around you all these years—it's catching."

"Yeah, well, remember, it's very dangerous to be funnier than the star."

"It may be dangerous—but it ain't difficult," Goldfarb squelched.

"Goldfarb, I'm gonna have you wired for silence. You drive the car and I'll tell the jokes. If I wanted a talker, I'd buy a parakeet—understand?"

"Yes, *sir*."

"Now, will you pick me up at two P.M.? Wake me at one. I'm going back to bed. Oh, before you go I want you to do something for me—just a minute."

Charlie wrote something on a piece of paper and

handed it to Goldfarb—he put his finger to his lips and pointed up. The note said: "Go down to the Pan Am Building and get me a reservation and a ticket for the 2:30 helicopter to Kennedy airport. Don't take the car and don't wear your uniform. Go out the side exit when you leave here —go by subway and make sure you are not being followed but don't make it obvious. If you understand—nod!"

Goldfarb nodded. Charlie scribbled some more: "No matter what I say to you from now on, ignore it—just do what the note says. Okay?" Goldfarb nodded again.

"Oh, Goldfarb," Charlie said, "you can have the morning off. Just bring me some cigars when you come back— and don't forget to wake me at one—"

"Yes, sir."

Charlie put up his hand and wrote again. "Go down and get my mail. I don't want it left at the door where anybody can pick it up. If it hasn't arrived yet—wait for it, but bring it up as soon as possible. I can't go to sleep until it's here—and when you come back in, open the door quietly, and don't talk—just hand me the mail. Nod if you understand."

Goldfarb nodded.

Fifteen minutes later he was back with the mail. He did look at Charlie a little peculiarly but he didn't say a word. He just handed him the letters and left.

Sure enough, there it was. The third letter from the top. He ripped open the envelope and held the filmed grenade in the palm of his hand. He stared at it for a moment, then put it in the breast pocket of his pajamas. He double-locked the door, turned off the phone and went to bed. He lay down with the happiest grin in weeks.

At exactly one o'clock Charlie jumped up like he had an alarm clock shoved up his nose. A minute later Goldfarb knocked on his bedroom door. "I'll be with you in ten minutes," Charlie shouted through the door. "Why don't you put some coffee on while I take a shower."

It was about fifteen minutes to two before Charlie finished dressing. The elevator took him down to the basement where Goldfarb was waiting with the Rolls. By the time they got to the Pan Am Building it was 2:15. Twenty minutes isn't bad to go from 64th and Fifth Avenue to 46th and Park in Barnes's traffic.

Goldfarb halted the car on the ramp side of the Pan Am Building and stepped out to open the door for the boss. "Wait for me," Charlie said grandly.

"Yes, sir."

With his cigar in one hand and the other hand free to wave at passers-by, he hurried into the building nodding and smiling at anything that moved.

He took the escalator up to the main lobby. Then took the elevator up to the 20th floor. He waited for the next elevator going down and took it to the 12th floor. From there he hitched a ride to the 18th and then down to the 6th. At exactly 2:25 he took the elevator down to the upper lobby, and stepped into the special elevator which takes you to the heliport on the 57th floor. Charlie was the last one on the helicopter. As soon as he was seated, the overhead propeller started to whirl and they were up and off.

The $8 ride took ten minutes. Round trip is only $10 but Charlie didn't intend to come back that way. He was playing it James Bond all the way. D.S. said to lose any tail. Well, he was so careful he wouldn't even cast a shadow.

The chopper dumped him at the Pan Am terminal at Kennedy at 2:41. At 2:50 he was in a taxi on his way to the RKO Theatre on 58th Street and Third Avenue. He purposely chose this movie house because it has two exits— 'The better to lose you, my dear.'

What he didn't count on was the picture playing. He

didn't even look at the marquee. He paid the admission and sat down in the last row of the theater so that he could case the whole joint at a glance. Only an hour to spend and then he was on his way to the appointment with Don Simon.

He suddenly looked up and saw Sean Connery carrying on like a maniac. He was driving his special car at 110 miles an hour; 007 pushed a button and a shield sprang up to ward off the bullets that were coming in his direction from the car following him; at the same time a smoke screen came out of the rear. He pressed another button and the girl sitting next to him was lifted out of the convertible and deposited on a passing tree. Another button and all kinds of nails and broken glass were distributed all over the road. When the Caddy following him blew a gasket and did a somersault while spitting out all kinds of flames, James Bond relaxed and slowed his machine to 95.

'Say,' Charlie made a mental note, 'I gotta get me one of those cars. I wonder if they come in a Rolls?'

At 4:30 Charlie walked out the side exit on 58th Street, west of Third Avenue. He walked to Lexington which is a one-way street and hailed a cab going downtown. He stopped at 49th and Lex, paid the driver and walked into the Bull and Bear restaurant of the Waldorf-Astoria, a few feet from the corner.

The Maitre d' greeted Charlie effusively, but our boy kept walking through the restaurant, up the few steps to the hotel entrance and onto the escalator, which took him to the lobby. He sauntered all the way across the foyer to the Park Avenue exit and quickly stepped into a cab that had conveniently unloaded four loaded conventioneers who looked like they were held over from a previous convention.

He drove two blocks in silence. Finally the cab driver spoke up. "Is it a secret where you're going, bud?"

Charlie came out of his trance. "Do you know where Teddy's is?" he asked.

"What is this, a quiz game? Or is that where you wanna go?"

"There are no straight men left," Charlie laughed. "Especially around a comic. There is something about us that brings out the cornball in them."

The driver turned around. "Milton Berle," he yelled. "Right? I'd know your voice anywhere. Boy, I never forget a face. I see you on TV all the time. Hey, the missus thinks you're the nuts. Personally I don't go for that kind of crap. I like them cowboy pictures. How come you never do cowboy pictures?"

It was too late for Charlie to change cabs. 'Anyway, he's insulting Berle, what's it to me?' he thought. 'Hey, that's the kind of crap I do.' Out loud he said, "Do you mind getting the lead out of your carburetor, pal? I've got to be at Teddy's at five o'clock."

"Look, pal," the man answered, "I don't tell you how to make jokes—stay out of my racket."

Sal Cuccinata, the owner of Teddy's, had arranged for Don Simon to be sitting in a booth under a picture of Charlie hugging his favorite TV ladies, Virginia Graham and Cindy Adams. Nothing puts the old boy in a better mood than facing himself. He greeted the picture, Don, and Sal in that order.

"I've been keeping your friend company," Sal said, "but I can't get him to eat anything."

"With this kind of food," Don said as he swallowed a shrimp scampi whole, "how does this man stay so thin?"

"Are you kidding?" Charlie said. "He doesn't eat here. He can't afford the prices. He gasses up at the Japanese steak joint next door—which he also happens to own."

"Which reminds me," Sal said, "I got to go over and check my Hibachi and Kobe steaks."

"I hate a smart ass," Charlie heckled. "Anyway, what's a nice Italian boy like you doing with a Jap joint? Before we know it you'll be serving Sukiyaki Parmigian."

Sal exited laughing like the perfect host that he is. He laughs at his guests, funny or not, never tops them, and leaves before he gets in the way.

"Well," Don asked when they were alone, "what's new?"

"I thought you'd never ask," Charlie answered. "For an opener, here's the microfilms of the entire communist spy movement in the U.S.A."

The F.B.I. man looked at him in disbelief. He held the film in the palm of his hand and just stared. "Any questions?" Charlie asked.

He carefully related the entire story, exactly as it happened, from the moment he left his apartment with the man-eating gorilla, his visit at Camp Comrade, his meeting with Marcee De Maye and the passing of the film, the mailing bit in Newburgh, Ina's assignment to spy on Sal De Maye and his broken-field running to get to Teddy's. The only thing he left out, of course, was his rendezvous with Barracuda Borkman. That remained a complete blackout. If he had to give his all for his country that was one thing, but he definitely refused to *tell* all.

"Well, now," Don said when he was all finished, "that's quite a story. If this film has what you say it has, you've done a big job for your country—you're a national hero."

"Yeah—and if they find out I'm the one that took it, I'll be the most popular stiff at Forest Lawn."

"I must say you've been lucky so far," Don said affectionately. "God certainly has been watching over you. But I must caution you to be extremely careful now—a wounded animal is the most dangerous."

"Don't worry," Charlie laughed, "I always look out for number one. I don't exactly hate myself, you know. I'm too beautiful to die. Now, where do we go from here?"

"Well," Don explained, "even if the film is authentic, we will still need the actual proof—we must catch them with the goods and we must get this De Maye to testify for us. We must get him to turn state's evidence."

"We?" he asked. "We? How do *we* do all this?"

The G man laid out his plan. For an hour Charlie listened as Simon explained in detail, step by step, operation Finko. He gave him a phone number that he could use "day or night—one of our operators will be there to answer it twenty-four hours a day.

"Now," he continued, "I have a little gift for you—a fountain pen." He handed him a light blue ballpoint.

"What is this—a Bar Mitzvah present?"

"This is a Jammer," he explained.

"Isn't that nice?" Charlie answered. "It's what I've always wanted. Now what the hell is a Jammer?"

"It jams all the bugs wherever you are. All you have to do is flip this clip and it knocks out any transmitter or receiving set in the immediate area."

"Say," Charlie said, "what a perfect way to shut up my mother-in-law."

"Do not take any chances. Even if you are in a restaurant, or a hallway—or the street. They can bug a sugar cube, or a tie tack. They can put a sending set in a pair of cuff links, earrings, or a wrist watch. They can transmit through a fountain pen or a ring—a martini, the flower in your lapel, a package of cigarettes—"

"How will I know—how do I recognize a bug?"

"You don't—that's why you must always use the Jammer if you don't want to be overheard. We could give you a gun—that is, a debugger—if you aim it in any direction and it emits a steady whining sound—that's the all clear signal. But if it stops sending sound, you know somebody has you tuned in."

"Why can't I have one of these guns?"

"It's too dangerous in case they catch you with it. How will you explain it? Besides, you really don't need it. Just turn on your Jammer when you don't want anybody listening in."

"Well, the least you could do is get me my very own sending set—how else am I supposed to get the message to you if somebody wants to kill me a little bit or something?"

"We have a sender for you—it's the newest and the most expensive made—it costs about twenty-five hundred. Now open your mouth."

"My mouth? What do you want to do—wire my tonsils?"

"Not exactly—but we can wire your teeth." He took a small oblong metal tube out of his vest pocket—about the size of a baby tooth. "When we insert this in one of your molars, you will be transmitting to one of our men who will always be within range of your beam."

"I got a bulletin for you. If you think you're going to take one of my beautiful teeth and stick a hole in it just to plant this—this—busybody in it, you're off your rocker. I've already given my body for the cause—but my teeth— never. Next you'll want to plant a midget with a headset in my kidney."

Simon laughed. "It's really not that bad," he said. "Let me see your mouth—" Charlie opened wide. "Ah—see you have a lower left molar that has a cap on it. All the dentist has to do is remove the cap and insert this—"

"Sure—why not remove all my teeth and put a television set in there?"

"This could be the difference between victory and failure, life and death. In order to follow through with our plan, we must be in communication with you at all times. At least, you must be able to reach us at any time—day or night. The phone is not always possible—there are too many ears listening—especially if you have to call from De Maye's house. This way, all you have to do is whisper and we're with you—"

"The life-and-death bit got to me," Charlie interrupted. "When, what, and where?"

"Tomorrow at one P.M.—Dr. Michaelson on Central Park South—here's the address. I purposely made it at one in the afternoon—I know you like to sleep late."

"You mean you had it set up all along? Suppose I didn't have a molar that was available? Suppose I didn't go for the whole bit?"

"You're too big a man to refuse."

"With that kind of logic how can I say no? Now I've got to get out of here. I know you'll miss me—don't pine too much. I'm still in showbusiness, you know. I haven't even talked to my writers or producer about what we are doing on the show this week or who's going to be on—"

"Go ahead," Simon said. "I'm staying here for dinner. We'll be in touch—and don't forget the dentist at one. He'll have the gadget."

"I'll be there. Before I go I better call Goldfarb. I told him to wait for me at the Pan Am Building—but that meant to wait a half-hour and go and then I'd call him and tell him where to meet me."

The maitre d' plugged a phone in at the table and Charlie called the mobile operator and gave his car number —it didn't answer. "That's funny," Charlie remarked, "Goldfarb wouldn't leave the car alone when he knows I'm going to call—I'll try the house." Nobody answered. Finally answering service came on—she hadn't heard from Goldfarb and there was no message for him or from him. He called Goldfarb's home—no answer. A call to the garage in his building only told him that the Rolls was there but no Goldfarb. No, he hadn't seen him come in; he came on duty at five and the car was already there.

"I can't understand it," Charlie mumbled aloud. "He never did anything like this before."

"I'm sure there must be some explanation," the G man suggested. "Like he went out to dinner, or he went to see his girl friend, or he was taken suddenly drunk—or—"

"Forget it," Charlie said. "Not Goldfarb. He doesn't drink, smoke, or go with broads—and if he eats, it's at the house."

"If the car is in the garage perhaps he's asleep upstairs and didn't hear the phone."

"Not a chance. He's never goofed off once in all the years he's worked for me. Except for the fact that he wants to be a comic—and hits me with my own jokes every once in a while—he's the perfect chauffeur."

"Well, maybe—"

"Maybe I ought to get home and see what's going on," Charlie interrupted. "You're as nervous as I am and you know it. What good is coking me up—" He got up to go.

"Look. If there is anything wrong call the number you have—we're only the snap of a finger away. Just make sure you use the code."

Charlie's mind was with Goldfarb when he stepped into the taxi in front of Teddy's. "Hey, Charlie Davis," the cab jockey threw at him, "I just been readin' aboutchew—that McHarry in duh *Nooze* called you a Pinko—and Oil Wilson in duh *Post* says you been playin' footsies wit dem lefties— I wood'n take that from nobody."

Even in the good days Charlie only heard compliments.

Now he was all eyes and ears for Goldfarb. "Thanks," he answered mechanically, "it's nice to hear it."

"Where yuh goin'?" the cabbie asked.

"TL 1-3113," he answered without hesitation and without thinking.

"Look, pal, I ain't gonna call yuh—I'm no operator, I'm a cab driver."

"Oh—uh—drop me at the Pan Am Building." He was still playing cops and robbers. He got out at the Park Avenue entrance, walked through to the ramp side and took a cab home from there, just in case they were watching for him at Pan Am, or somebody questioned the cabbie when he got home and wanted to know where he picked him up.

The ten-second flight to the 20th floor was like ten hours for Charlie. 'They wouldn't dare touch Goldfarb,' he kept thinking. 'Haven't I co-operated with them and that degenerate female gorilla especially, but what if they grab him to insure my job with De Maye—they did it before with the blonde and Marcee's brother. If they harm one hair of Goldfarb's head—I'll—aaaah, Simon is right—maybe he just went out for a minute to run an errand, he must be back by now. Could they have followed us to the Pan Am and suspected something when I didn't return? Maybe they grabbed Goldfarb to get him to tell them where I went. If I know Goldfarb, he'd die before he'd tell them anything. They could kill him at that—life means nothing to these bastards. If . . .'

Charlie inserted the key in the lock and entered his apartment. He turned the wall switch on; instead of light, darkness came. He thought the whole building fell on him. That first klop on the head was more pain than he could collect in a lifetime. His head felt like a grenade during the explosion. He was holding onto the floor for dear life when the second klop came and the merciful blackout.

He was dropping—dropping—dropping into space, black space, through the clouds and finally into the sunshine —flying alongside the plane—no matter how much he tried, he couldn't open the door and get inside the plane. His arms were heavy—

Now he was in Las Vegas MCing the show. The girls on stage were wearing *Naughty Marietta* outfits, completely covered from head to foot, and the audience was all in the nude. He was wearing a full dress suit, high hat and all, but his suit was cut out from the waist to his knees. He was doing his magic act, sawing a woman in half—it was Ina Borkman. He tried and tried but the saw couldn't get through her—she kept grabbing at his tools.

He finally called on a man in the audience to help him —it was LBJ. Together they sawed her in half, only what came out wasn't blood—it was borscht. The borscht was freezing cold and it kept spraying his face—it felt great. . . .

When he opened his eyes, Goldfarb was caressing his head and face with an ice bag. "Wh-what happened?" Charlie mumbled.

"I don't know what happened to you," Goldfarb answered. "I heard the door open and then a crash—"

"That was my head—"

"I was tied up in the kitchen—it took me two hours to get loose but I finally made it—and here I am."

"You mean I've been lying here for two hours?"

"You must have been on the floor for two hours— you've been in bed for three. It's midnight. Doctor Gilbert just left—he said you'll be okay, he said it's lucky you got a stone head."

"Help me sit up, will you? Ow—oooh—oiy—what happened to the lights? Will somebody please cut my head off —oiy—oiy oiy . . ."

"What were they looking for, Mr. Davis? They didn't

touch your jewelry or your clothes, or many of your antiques, but the house is a wreck. They cut it to pieces. They certainly were searching for something—they turned everything inside out—"

"My gag file—did they get my gag file?" Charlie asked a little hysterically.

"Are you kidding, Mr. Davis? That's petty larceny. These jokers were looking for something important."

"What do you want to be—a comedian or something?"

"Yeah, don't you?"

"One more joke and you're fired."

"One more joke and I quit—even with a dented funny bone, you're still the greatest, Mr. Davis."

"You're hired—now tell me what happened."

"Well, when I dropped you off at the Pan Am Building I waited a half-hour like you said, then I drove back here to the house to get a bite to eat and wait for your call—but don't worry, I didn't eat much—"

"It's all counted—it'll come off your salary. Now stop with the jokes and tell me what happened."

"Anyway, the doorman rang and said there was a gentleman downstairs with a manuscript for Mr. Davis from United Artists and that the man insisted that somebody in the apartment must sign for it.

"When I opened the door for him, instead of a manuscript the man had a gun in his hand. I couldn't think of a funny line so I let him in. It's tough to ad-lib with a .38.

"The nice young man then took me to the kitchen, tied me up with our own cord yet, put a tape over my mouth and took himself some Diet-Rite cola from the fridge.

"A few minutes later I heard the house phone buzz. The man answered and said, 'Okay, tell them to come up.' Then I heard the three of them talking in the living room. After a few minutes the door opened and shut and the little man left—I knew it was my friend because the two voices that remained were different from the sweet boy with the gun who bound me up so gently and securely."

"Did you get a look at those two?"

"No, but I'd know their voices anywhere—I had my back toward them but I could feel the hate on the face of the darling little man who promised to cut off my manhood if I didn't tell him where you went after I dropped you at the Pan Am Building—or where you stashed some kind of film."

"So how come they didn't operate—or couldn't they find it?" Charlie asked.

"No, the other charmer said something about some comrade who wouldn't like it if they messed up your apartment—"

"That's true," Charlie agreed. "It wouldn't be neat having you spread out all over the place."

Charlie knew who the Katzenjammer Kids were but he had to make sure. He called the doorman. Yes, one was a blond and the other looked like Edward G. Robinson with the longest arms he ever saw. No, he didn't remember their names but he said they asked for Goldfarb and *Goldfarb said to* send them up. Then he called Ina Borkman.

"I told you," Ina Borkman said, "not to call me here unless it was an extreme emergency!"

"Well," Charlie answered, "would you say cutting out my chauffeur's personal belongings is an extreme emergency? Let alone my life, which is fairly important—especially to me."

"I'm sorry about that," Ina said feelingly. "It was all a horrible mistake—"

"If you think I got it—why are you asking me to try to find out where it is? I really don't get the whole bit—when do I pass?"

"I promise it won't happen again. It was not my orders —they did it on their own. They were only supposed to protect you. When you were missing they got a little panicky. The search and the physical job was their own idea—it won't happen again, I promise you. You mean too much to us— to me!"

"You certainly have a great way of showing it."

"I showed it to you the other day, didn't I?" she cooed.

"No comment—but I do have a message for Hansel and Gretel. Tell them I just bought a .38, and if they ever come near me or anybody connected with me for any reason, I will give them each an extra navel."

The next day Charlie went to see Dr. Michaelson to get himself fitted to talk through his teeth. He spent the rest of the week working on his TV show for Saturday night. As it turned out, it was the best show of the season. Like I always said, a bump on the head brings out the best in you, if you happen to be a comedian—and I should know—should know—should know—should know. . . .

Charlie called Marcee after his show. "Mr. Davis," she squealed, "I just saw you on television—you were wonderful."

"When did you get back?" he asked.

"Today," she answered. "I got two days off for good behavior."

"Wonderful," he said. "How about joining me for dinner tonight?"

"I'd love it."

And a good time was had by all. Like they say on the Borscht Belt, "Why not?" He was ready, she was willing, and his apartment was empty. He turned his jammer on and they jammed all night.

The next night they spent in *her* home. Like it says in

all the joke books, they figured let *her* father worry. Now he turned his jammer on for a different reason—the big summit meeting between Marcee, her father, and himself.

Sal De Maye was willing to turn state's evidence. He would hand over all the original files, lock, stock, and fingerprints to the F.B.I. "Only how do I know my little girl will be safe?" was all he wanted to know.

"She'll be in the bosom of the F.B.I. We don't make a move until we get the signal that she's safe and sound."

"And how about me?" he asked humbly.

"I got to level with you," Charlie said. "They can't promise you anything except a square deal—but if I know my Uncle Sam, he's one relative that will never let you down."

"That's good enough for me," Sal said. "Even an American jail would be better than the prison I've been in since they first brought me to this country. I feel free at last."

It was after one o'clock in the morning when Charlie finished setting up their plans. Goldfarb was waiting in front of the house in the Rolls. As soon as the car pulled away from the curb, Charlie called the special number. "The preview went fine," he said. "The personal appearance is scheduled for tomorrow afternoon. My sponsor has given me an open-door policy but no time to rehearse. My new teeth should make a big difference. Believe it or not, it not only feels better but the new look gives me more confidence. The star is in good voice and ready to sing his heart out."

The car had been debugged earlier but Charlie was taking no chances. Especially since Don Simon had warned him time and again to use double-talk code at all times.

Translated, the message was: "De Maye is co-operating all the way. He'll give us names, places, and dates. The fink is coming with the papers tomorrow sometime after twelve noon. The front door will be unlocked—I'll tell you through the gadget in my teeth when you can enter—De Maye tells me you will have only a few minutes to grab him—he rarely stays longer than that—but I got confidence in you, and remember the Marcee plan."

Charlie didn't even stop off for a short bow at the Stage or Morocco—talk about sacrifices. He was going to try to get some sleep. He had to get up at the crack of 11 A.M. and he wanted to be alert for the big finale.

The TV truck was sitting at the curb opposite the De Maye house when Charlie walked up the steps of the brownstone building at exactly 11:45. He rang the doorbell and was greeted by Marcee with a nervous hug. "I was just leaving," she said. "I have an appointment for a new job—do I look nice?"

"If I told you you had a beautiful body," he leered, "would you hold it against me?"

"You know it," she answered as she started down the steps. The taxi appeared from nowhere. Charlie walked her to the cab and opened the door. "Take care of my girl," Charlie said to the driver as he handed him a couple of bucks.

"Don't worry," Don Simon said, "she's in good hands."

Charlie rang the bell for the second time. Now Sal De Maye himself welcomed him. Charlie went in and unlatched the lock as he shut the door.

"Hi," he said, "I just saw Marcee to a cab. She tells me she is on her way to a new job. Now you can retire," he laughed.

"Not yet," De Maye answered. Charlie's tooth was turned on and they were talking to the G men in the TV truck across the street. "My daughter has been unhappy with her work lately. I hope this turns out right for her. She said she'd call me as soon as she was accepted. I'm so anxious, I won't be able to do a stitch of work till I hear from her."

To the F.B.I. he was saying: "I'll go all the way as soon

as I know my girl is safe—but not before." To anybody else listening, he was just a father concerned about his daughter.

"Oh," Charlie remembered, "Marcee told me your TV set was on the blink. I told Harry Heller to get in touch with you. He does all the work for the station. He's the best TV repairman in the business—and he's not a robber."

"He was here earlier," De Maye said, "but I told him to come back later when my mind was clearer."

"It's not your mind that has to be cleared up, it's your screen," Charlie answered. "I don't care about anybody else, but I want to look good in this house—I'm too beautiful to be distorted."

De Maye laughed. "Thanks," he said. "This is the first time I've laughed in months."

"That's pretty insulting," Charlie said. "You told me you watch my show every week, and you haven't laughed in months? Thanks a lot. I forgot to tell you, I do comedy, you know."

"You're wonderful," De Maye laughed.

"I admire your taste." Now they were discussing his very favorite subject—which was a cue for a half-hour lecture on Charlie Davis, the star, given by nobody else but the big man himself. Once he got started on that kick nothing outside of murder or the telephone could stop him.

Mr. De Maye picked up the phone on the first ring. "I got the job," Marcee said right off.

"Do you like it?" Pop asked.

"Very much."

"I mean is the boss nice?"

"He couldn't be sweeter!"

"What kind of place is it—is it a pleasant office and everything?"

"It's lovely—I'm the only girl with four men in one office—what more can a girl ask?"

"Good," Mr. De Maye said. "Now I can relax—as long as my baby is set."

"Don't worry, Daddy," she said. "I'm in very good hands."

He repeated the whole conversation to Charlie. "Now I can do what I have to do," he added.

Charlie turned on his Jammer fountain pen and turned up the radio. "When do you expect the fink with the plans for our new atomic planes?"

"He should be here any minute now. This is his day off at the plant and he usually gets here between twelve and one —it's almost one now."

Charlie turned off the radio and the fountain pen and turned on his molar. "Well," he called out, "it's one o'clock and all's well. See? I bet you never thought when you opened the door for me this morning you would have your own town crier. Any minute now the bad weather man will show up— so you better hurry and get your TV set fixed. How else will you know if we're having any weather?"

To the F.B.I. men in the TV truck this meant, "The coast is clear, the door is open, and the fink is on his way. So get the hell over here immediately."

Thirty seconds later the two G men were in the house. Both were dressed like TV repairmen. The white man was about five feet ten inches. He was wearing coveralls over a dark plaid shirt and a peak cap. He had a tool chest slung over his shoulder on a long leather strap.

The other man was the Negro letter carrier who had brought Charlie the message from Don Simon. He was all togged out in a dirty pair of brown trousers, a dark blue sweater with short sleeves, and a straw hat that looked like some horse was glad to get rid of it.

"Where's the set?" the letter carrier wanted to know.

"In here," Mr. De Maye said.

Charlie turned on his Jammer as the boys showed him their identification. He remembered the colored F.B.I. agent's name was Bart Rackback. The other one's card spelled out Harry Guttenberg.

"I put the lock back on," Rackback said, "so your visitor will have to ring the bell. Now, where do you usually transact your business?"

"In this room," De Maye answered. "He gives me the papers and I take pictures of them—then I return the papers to him and he leaves—it never takes more than a few minutes."

"Okay," Guttenberg said. "Let's get out of sight. Mr. Davis, will you go into the next room—don't go far, we'll need you as a witness. Bart and I will be behind the drapes. Now, Mr. De Maye, when the bell rings just make sure you bring him in here as usual, and don't take the papers from him until you are here in this room. Is that understood?"

"Yes, sir."

"And Mr. Davis—don't come in until we call you!"

"Okay."

Rackback placed his own Jammer on the coffee table just to play it safe. There was no time to test the room with his debugger and he didn't want to rely on Charlie's Jammer in the other room.

Everybody took up their posts to wait for the pigeon. Rackback and Guttenberg behind the drapes, Charlie in the next room and De Maye on the sofa waiting for the bell to ring.

Fifteen minutes later they were still waiting for something to happen. By one-thirty they were starting to get a little restless. The G men were pretty hot under the drapes and Charlie was beginning to get nervous waiting to make his entrance.

When the star hadn't shown by two o'clock, De Maye

said to the drapes: "He was never this late before—maybe he's not coming."

Charlie hollered in from the other room, "Do you think they were tipped and stopped him? Maybe the Jammer isn't working—maybe they saw you come in—maybe . . ."

"Please don't talk at all now," Rackback said, "not until we give you the signal. It's still early—please don't make any sound—please."

At 2:20 the bell rang. Even though they were waiting for it, it caught the four inmates of the De Maye home by surprise. Charlie jumped like he was kicked by a sponsor, De Maye came off the couch like he bounced off a trampoline. Rackback whispered to De Maye, "Take it nice and easy."

"Sorry I'm late," the man said as he came in. "I've been riding the subway for hours—I had a funny feeling I was being followed. I'm going to have to stay away for a little while—take a trip. Do you have my money?"

"Sure—here," De Maye said.

The man reached into his inside jacket pocket and pulled out the papers and handed them to De Maye.

The camera flashed and Rackback said, "Don't move, you're under arrest—Federal Bureau of Investigation." The .38 he held in his hand convinced the man they weren't playing hide-and-seek—he froze.

Guttenberg held the camera in one hand and a gun in the other. "Mr. Davis, would you join us?" Rackback flashed his credentials to the fink. "Now, sir, will you please put the papers and that envelope on the table?"

The man did as he was told. "Now please raise your hands." He frisked him for a weapon but all he could come up with was his wallet and identification. Rackback counted the money in the man's wallet and showed it to Davis and De Maye. He also showed them the name and address on his

Social Security card, then he examined the money in the white envelope De Maye had handed him. And the papers that the fink had brought in. He asked De Maye and Charlie to witness it all.

"Now," Guttenberg said to the man, "will you please change clothes with me?" The man didn't say word number one, he just followed orders. He was about the same height as Guttenberg—maybe an inch shorter. He was about ten pounds heavier but it was all in his behind.

He removed his homburg hat, dark gray herringbone suit and vest, as well as his black shoes, shirt and tie. Standing there in his underwear and socks and thick glasses like the bottom of milk bottles, he looked like something out of Mars that they were very happy to get rid of.

He put on the dark plaid shirt, coveralls and peak cap that Guttenberg had discarded. "You may wear your own shoes," the G man told him.

When they were both finished dressing, Guttenberg slung the tool chest over the fink's shoulder. "Now you are going to leave here with my partner, cross the street and get into that TV truck. There are six guns trained on you from inside the truck and we have twelve other men on the street ready for any emergency. I would suggest that you just act natural—any false move and Mr. Rackback would be only too happy to put a couple of holes in your legs."

"And you won't need these." Rackback removed the fink's glasses. "You'll get them back when you are safely in custody."

Guttenberg watched from the window while the two men crossed the street and got into the front of the truck and drove away.

"What's the gimmick?" Charlie asked. "Why the masquerade? Are they going on 'To tell the truth' or what?"

"In case anybody is watching," the G man said, "we

don't want to make any waves until we tie it all up. This way it looks like the two TV repairmen that came in earlier left the same way. We don't want to scare them away from the big pay-off.

"Meanwhile I'll be here to handle this situation until I get relieved, which should be any minute. Then I'll take a taxi wearing his clothes and glasses.

"Two men from the department will be here to take Mr. De Maye and all his files into custody, and don't worry about a thing—this whole block is completely surrounded with Government men."

"Well, how about me?" Charlie asked.

"You deliver the microfilm," Guttenberg explained, "that Mr. De Maye will make of these papers. We can't let De Maye make the delivery—he's too valuable right now."

"I get it," Charlie said, "*I'm* expendable. You mean it doesn't matter if *I* get a bullet up my crotch now—I'm a has-been—right?"

"Not at all," the F.B.I. man smiled. "We'll have you covered with six cars and over thirty men. We're depending on you for the big finish."

"Did you say *my* finish?"

The bell rang. De Maye ushered in two handsome young men who could have been actors, lawyers, or Madison Avenue executives. Their cards said they were Martin Murphy and Bill Bartell of the Federal Bureau of Investigation.

Guttenberg turned the De Maye household over to the newest G men and stepped out into the outside world, dressed as the fink of the year, and into a cab that just "happened" to be passing by.

Charlie was now full of code besides a lot of other things, for he was now briefed by the F.B.I. as well as the Reds, and now he had this delivery to make from the fink to De Maye to the shoeshine boy. 'But even Tinkers-to-Eversto-Chance sometimes got screwed up, and they were pros,' he thought.

"I hope," he said to Murphy and Bartell, "my delivery will be as good as Dennis Day's wife—you see, Mrs. Day had ten children and—oh, forget it, I'm not myself today— you notice the improvement?"

They smiled politely. "Look," he said, "if anything happens to me, return Milton Berle's gag file and tell him I died on my own."

The F.B.I. knew he was making the pass. So did the Reds. But Charlie was so spy-happy by now that he took a cab to 86th Street and Lexington Avenue, then a crosstown bus to Central Park West and from there to 50th and Eighth Avenue by subway and a taxi to the Drecker Hotel on East 35th Street—a block away from the De Maye home.

The barbershop was in the basement of the hotel. The shoeshine stand was in a little room by itself just inside the shop with three high chairs. On the opposite wall was a series of hooks for hats and coats. The shine boy was putting a jacket on a customer and brushing him off when Charlie came in and sat down on one of the high chairs.

"Can I get a shine without getting a haircut and shave?" he asked, as he had been briefed by De Maye.

"Why not?" was the answer he expected.

"Well," he stuck to the script, "I want one of your special shines—I want to see my face in it."

"Whose face do you expect to see?" Now they were squared away.

Charlie watched the boy as he worked on his shoes. He was about twenty-five years old—approximately 5 feet 9 inches tall, curly black hair, big broad shoulders, a handsome clear face with the smoothest skin he had ever seen on a man. What a waste of American.

In spite of the manly look and the bass voice, Charlie

thought: 'He's a queen. I could spot those limp wrists at twenty paces. I wouldn't want to turn my back on him for many reasons—I bet he'd be more trouble than Borkman.'

You could never fool Charlie with the gay set. He had worked with too many chorus boys and been propositioned too many times to make a mistake. 'Say,' he thought, 'I'm lucky at that—imagine if this fag took me up to Camp Comrade instead of Borkman. Not me, that's one place I stop—I'd give up my citizenship first.'

"Okay," the boy said, "can you see your face in it?"

"Beautiful," Charlie answered. "What do I owe you?"

"Twenty-five cents—you pay the cashier," he said, handing him a tab.

"Thank you." Charlie smiled as he gave him a half dollar. It was the biggest tip he had ever received. Inside the fifty-cent piece were the plans for the atomic plane that De Maye had put on microfilm and inserted in the trick coin.

Charlie walked up the steps to the lobby and out the swinging doors. The cab he hailed was there as he lifted his finger. "Where to?" Don Simon asked.

"Indonesia," Charlie answered.

"Sukarno is having enough trouble," he smiled. "How did it go?"

"Fine," Charlie said. "Comes the revolution, everybody will be shining shoes."

"Did he suspect anything?"

"Are you kidding? With my acting? I dazzled him with my footwork. I acted so good he didn't even recognize me —the son of a bitch."

Simon drove him around the corner where the car was waiting. "You know what this bug looks like—follow him," Don explained. "We have six moving vehicles all with two-way radios, and thirty men on foot. As soon as you spot our victim coming out of the hotel just tell me and it will be transmitted to all the other vehicles and they will get it to our men in the street. We also have two men in the Thirty-fourth Street subway—one on the uptown and one on the downtown side. We can't lose him. We've got to be there when he makes the pass."

Simon got out of the cab and into the back of the car with Charlie. Another man got out of the car and took the wheel of the cab. The man driving the car for Charlie and Don was as nondescript as the car.

The whole move took a couple of minutes, from the time Charlie left the Drecker to the time he returned. "The hotel only has three exits and they are all alongside each other," Simon explained. "The revolving door and the straight door from the lobby, and the employee and delivery entrance right next to it. See?—those steps leading up from the basement? . . ."

"No back entrances?"

"None—we checked it all out. Here! Put these glasses on, and the hat, in case he glances into the car as he comes out."

I got a little news for you. Don't fool around with Gene Autry or the F.B.I. These boys sure are thorough. The horn-rimmed black spectacles didn't have any glass in them but the hat was a perfect fit in spite of the fact that Charlie never wore a hat in his life.

"We have a fairly good description of him. One of our boys checked him while you were getting your shine," Simon told Charlie. "Of course, you were able to observe him at closer range—but remember, he might be wearing a different suit or hat or glasses . . ."

"I'd know this bum," Charlie sneered, "if he were dressed up as Santa Claus."

It was five o'clock and the employees were starting to leave the hotel through the side door. The main entrance had plenty of action. Charlie kept his eyes glued to the three exits.

It was still light out, but with the rush of traffic at that hour, Charlie had his eyes full. Two or three times he tensed when he thought he recognized his patsy coming out of the employees' exit, but at second glance it turned out to be three other guys.

It was getting dark now and a little tougher to discern the figures coming out of the hotel.

"What time is it?" Charlie asked without looking away from the three exits.

"Six-fifty-five."

"Do you think we could have missed him while we drove around the corner?"

"No, we had a couple of men here who had his description—anyway, it was only a couple of minutes."

"Maybe he's not coming out at all. Maybe he passed it to somebody else in the hotel."

"I don't think that's possible. We have a man on him. Of course, we can't take the chance of scaring him away, but De Maye says he always delivers himself. Are you sure *you* didn't miss him?"

"Positive. If I miss this bum, I'll tear up Erle Stanley Gardner's phone number. I never—" Charlie grabbed the G man's arms: "Hold it—that's him all right—it's him!"

"Which one—where?"

"The beatnik with the long black hair down to his shoulders. See him with the guitar?—and the sneakers? He just came out of the revolving doors—"

"Are you sure?" Simon was on the phone.

"Of course I'm sure. I'd know that friggin' fag if he were in drag. Now come on—follow him."

Simon was broadcasting the description to all the operators—in trucks, cars, motorcycles, walkie-talkies, and the tiny transistors the foot operators were tuned to. Operation Finko was in full swing.

The car was parked on 35th Street, which is a one-way street going west. The shoeshine boy was walking east.

Don called for the car that was nearest to take over. In case he grabbed a vehicle while they made the trip around the block for the pick-up.

"Are you sure?" Don Simon asked again. "How did you spot him?"

"The walk—he walks lightly, like Berle or Hope when they're camping. And the sneakers—they're not filthy."

"I don't get it."

"Did you ever see a beatnik with clean sneakers? They can be stoned for having a box of Ajax in their home. You can be thrown out of their union just for taking a bath."

"I know, but—"

"Furthermore," Charlie continued, "did you notice he carried the guitar by the neck? No musician would do that. In the first place he would have a cover for it.

"Another thing. That wasn't make-up on his hands—it was shoe polish."

"Very good deductions," Simon said sincerely.

"Elementary, my dear Simon," Charlie smiled. "He couldn't fool me if he stretched his hair or shrunk his head— that wig looks like it *belongs* on a horse's ass."

"There he is," Simon said as they turned the corner. The Red fink was swishing along like he didn't have a care in the world or the plans in his pocket.

"It's flying around like he's got it made."

"Don't worry about a thing," Simon answered. "We got him covered like a blanket—we couldn't lose him if he flew away."

Watching the F.B.I. tailing a pigeon is like viewing a work of art. No man shadows him for more than a couple of blocks at a time, in case he turns around or happens to glance in that direction. The moving vehicles keep taking over for each other according to the traffic and the situation.

The shoeshine boy walked to First Avenue, made a left turn and continued his prance uptown, totally unaware of the live chess game going on around him.

He led the parade up First Avenue to 40th Street, then left to Lexington and right to 42nd Street. He stopped off at a little coffee shop called Oggie's.

The block was surrounded immediately. When the Red menace sat down at the counter he was joined by a tall Negro in workmen's clothes. A minute later a sailor walked in and took a seat on the other side of him three stools away. Could this be the big pass, Charlie thought, in a coffee shop?

The workman ordered a Danish and coffee. The sailor wanted a glass of milk and a Swiss cheese sandwich. They never once looked in the direction of the man they were tailing. The instant beatnik asked for coffee.

He nursed his java for about ten minutes and then ordered another. He kept looking at his watch every once in a while like he was waiting for somebody or just marking time.

The two F.B.I. men finished their food and asked for their checks and left—but not before two gentlemen came in together and occupied stools at the end of the counter nearest the door. From their conversation, they were in the publishing business and in New York on a convention. They kept telling each other jokes like regular Bennett Cerfs and screaming at the gags—but at no time was the Commie out of sight or sound.

It wasn't until the third set of G men took over that the pigeon decided to fly. He snuck a dime under the plate, paid the check for his three coffees with a dollar bill, got his change and left.

The giant shadow spread out again. Obviously he had

been killing time and now he was on his way. Operation Finko sprang to life once more.

He looked at his watch for the hundredth time. It was 8:20. He obviously had no idea he was being followed. He was so sure of his disguise and so confident he was free and clear that he didn't even bother to play hide-and-seek.

Apparently it was time for his appointment. He hailed a cab and directed him to the Rose Cole Art Galleries on 57th Street between Fifth and Madison. This was too easy. The taxi was one of the F.B.I.'s. The G man driving repeated the address so that Simon and the others could hear it and then turned off his radio.

This gave Don and Charlie a chance to enter the gallery before the pigeon so that it would not seem that he had a following. Three other agents got there ahead of the beatnik —a man and woman that looked like they were on their honeymoon shopping for their new apartment, and a distinguished-looking gentleman who could have been an heir to millions.

Charlie added a mustache to go with his spectacles and Simon wore dark glasses. They took seats in the back of the room. The couple sat in the center to the right side and the heir took up his post left and front.

The room was almost half full—about seventy people. The auctioneer was asking for bids on a black canvas with one little yellow dot on the right-hand corner. He called it "Dark Painting" and it sure was. "My house painter could do better. My nephew who is five years old could make a nicer dot," Charlie whispered to Simon.

The first bid was 30,000 dollars. "Thirty thousand?" Charlie repeated. "Thirty thousand? I wouldn't give him thirty dollars *with* the frame and a picture of the painter in the nude thrown in, even if the painter was Brigitte Bardot."

"Shhh—quiet," Simon warned.

And the auctioneer was insulted yet. "Folks," he said condescendingly, "thirty thousand for a genuine, original Gutterman?"

"Original?" Charlie whispered. "Who the hell would want to copy it?"

"Shut up," Simon said between his teeth.

"Forty thousand," said the bald-headed patron in front of Charlie.

"Fifty thousand," said a voice up front.

"Barnum was wrong. Suckers aren't born every minute," Charlie mumbled. "These suckers are bidding faster than that."

Charlie wasn't sure if the "Dark Painting" sold for 70 or 75 thousand. The shoeshine boy entered when it hit about 56 grand. He stood in the back of the auditorium for about five or six minutes casually looking over the proceedings. He finally made up his mind and nonchalantly strolled down the center aisle and sat down in the fifth row next to—

"That's Ina Borkman," Charlie almost exploded. "I didn't notice her until now. He sat down next to Borkman."

"Shhh—I know, I know," Simon whispered. "I saw her when we came in. We got somebody on her. He's sitting two rows behind. Now will you please shut up—*please*."

Now there were at least twelve sets of eyes watching the fink and the finkess. Another set parked themselves in back of them.

The boy and the monster never looked at each other once. She didn't even glance up when he sat down. They both just stared straight ahead like they were entranced with the paintings being auctioned off by the glorified pitchman.

Somebody by the name of Jubey Traum or Juddey Traum "stole" a painting called "Wheat." It was a real burlap bag, torn, tacked on a plain canvas. Mr. Traum outbid the other patrons by offering $80,000 for this gem. "I would have to get some painter to fix this up—before I threw it away," Charlie mumbled.

Simon left Charlie and joined the new eyes behind the two finks.

The artistic con man was asking for bids on a piece of cracked cement that was surrounded by a hand-carved frame. "What am I bid for this B. Shnaider?" he said like he was offering Mia Farrow Sinatra's solitaire.

'Is he kidding?' Charlie said to himself. 'Even the sidewalk was glad to get rid of it.' It sold for $27,000.

Somebody named Simon Michaelson had a picture made up of old theater tickets, programs, and Raleigh coupons. "A bargain," the spieler said, "at twenty-five thousand."

The only one that got the bargain was Simon Michaelson. Some yutz paid the 25 grand.

"I beg your pardon," Borkman turned to the shoeshine boy, "I have to make a phone call and I don't have a dime—can you give me change of a dollar, please?"

"Sure," the boy said, "if I got it." He reached in his jacket and pulled out a handful of change. He offered her two dimes, a nickel, a quarter and—*the* half dollar. As soon as she put it all in her purse, Simon said quietly in her ear, "Federal Bureau of Investigation." He stuck his identification in front of her. "I'll have your purse, please," he said as he quickly picked it up.

The shoeshine boy started to get up. "I wouldn't if I were you," the G man next to Simon said as he put a pair of handcuffs on him. The man sitting two rows behind Borkman was there now and gave Ina her very own shiny bracelets.

"What's this all about?" Ina asked innocently. "Does everybody get handcuffed because they change a dollar bill?"

"They do if the change carries American secret plans to the enemy."

"If this is some kind of joke," she said bitterly, "I don't think it's very funny. I'll talk to my Congressman about this."

"We'd appreciate that very much," Simon answered. "Now I think we'd better be going. And I suggest that you go quietly."

"You can't treat me this way," she sputtered. "I'm a good citizen. . . ."

"Of what country?" he asked.

Charlie took his mustache and glasses off as Borkman passed with Simon & Co. "Charlie Davis," she hollered when she spotted him. "Charlie darling, tell them they're making a mistake. Tell them who I am."

"Sure," Charlie obeyed. "She's a dirty lecherous old Red bastard who ought to be strung up by her libido."

"Drop dead," she spit.

"After you, madame," he bowed, opening the door for her. "And I use the term advisedly."

Charlie was propped up in bed with a cold bottle of imported champagne in one hand and a hot local broad in the other . . . watching the "11 o'clock news" on WABC-TV with Cindy Adams and John Schubeck.

"This was the greatest roundup of Communist spies in history," Cindy was saying. "Over one hundred and thirty Reds were trapped by the F.B.I. with the help of comedian Charlie Davis. John . . ."

"Sal De Maye," Schubeck continued, "former key party member, has turned state's evidence and turned over all his secret documents to the F.B.I. This can put scores of Russian agents in jail for the rest of their lives.

"They say he switched when the party killed his own son who wanted to bolt the hammer and sickle. Roy Darvis and Dirk Jones are being held for the murder of young De

Maye as well as a blonde model named Candy Sweets and dozens of others revealed in the files of De Maye's vaults. Cindy . . ."

"According to a high police official," Cindy took over, "they have the murder weapons and the fingerprints of the communist killers. The big catch, however, was Ina Borkman, the super-spy who was the head of the entire operation, and an American scientist, B. Richard Rudin. John . . ."

"The F.B.I.," John carried on, "has only the greatest admiration for famous comedian Charlie Davis who was responsible for breaking the back of the entire spy ring while working for the Federal Bureau of Investigation. As Charlie Davis put it, 'I was a comic for the F.B.I.' WABC's Cindy Adams talked to Charlie Davis only an hour ago, right after the roundup. Cindy . . ."

"Charlie," Marcee squealed, "that's you on the screen. It's you!"

"Sure, baby. The whole country is watching me, but you got me. And if you're a good girl you may get an encore."

"I must pay my respects to the F.B.I.," Charlie was saying to Cindy Adams on the screen. "I couldn't have done it without them. They were a big help to me."

"I'm sure," Cindy said, "Mr. Hoover will be happy to hear that."

The phone rang—and rang—and rang.

"Why don't you answer it?" Marcee asked.

"Goldfarb will," he answered. "It's probably the papers. I'd rather not talk to anybody tonight."

Goldfarb knocked on the door and entered. "It's Joe Levine. He said it's very important. He must talk to you right away."

"Every producer in the country will want to do my life story now," he bragged. "If Levine wants me he'll have to pay. At least a million and a percentage of the picture. At least fifty per cent. If they want me they will have to get it up. Just listen to the kid operate."

Charlie picked up the phone. "Yes, Joe," he started coldly.

"I think that's a good title for a picture," Levine said. " 'I Was A Comic For The F.B.I.' I heard the news on ABC. I'd like one of my writers to talk to you about the entire episode. It will make a great picture."

"Let's get it straight," Charlie said. "I'll write it myself. And I'll direct. And remember, I get billed *over* the picture. It's Charlie Davis *in* 'I Was A Comic For The F.B.I.' Do I make myself clear?"

"I don't think you understand," Mr. Levine said quietly. "I don't want you to play yourself on the screen. This is a perfect vehicle for Milton Berle."

"Berle?" he shouted into the phone. "Berle? I'm the guy who lived through it. It's my life. My story. What's the matter with me playing it?"

"You're not the type," Levine said as he hung up.

Charlie stared at the phone for a couple of seconds, shrugged his shoulders and replaced the phone in the cradle. "Put out the lights," he said to Marcee. "We'll show 'em who's the star."

THE SWINGERS

I promised it would be the swingingest affair of the year. With the guests June and I had assembled for our homecoming from Southeast Asia, the party at our house had to be a killer—and that's just how it turned out. But I'm getting ahead of my story.

An invitation to spend an evening with the Dan Masons is like a Command Performance with the "in" people of our town. It's not that I'm bragging. I don't have to do that anymore. I've been a comedian, writer, producer, and director for years. I was born a star. At first I had to fight my way to convince one and all I was the greatest. But that was the time I was campaigning to get to the top. . . . Now that I'm a proven commodity and a world-wide celebrity, I don't have to show off anymore. Don't misunderstand, I'm still the greatest. It's just that I'm more humble about it.

My beautiful and talented wife June who promised to love, honor, and applaud when she took my name fifteen years ago may have forgotten most of the promises, but she did keep the name June Mason and attracted her own disciples as an expert on Asian affairs when she did a series on Oriental potentates for *World Magazine*.

Everybody showed up at the party. They had to. It was like a status symbol to be at a Dan Mason affair. Those who did not get invited were "out." Those who showed up were "in." There was the handsome Barbara Blaze, the Number One best-selling authoress of the dirtiest book of the century, *The Pill Takers*. Barbara was holding court in one corner of the living room, explaining that "You don't have to be a call girl or a tramp to write about them. I never took dope, but I can write about the dolls. Look at Edgar Wallace. He wrote the Tarzan series and he never set foot in Africa."

"Sure," Irene Gardner was meowing on the other side of the room. "She wrote the book while she was head of a Girl Scout troop. And that June Mason. You mean to tell me she didn't have to lay down a little on those Oriental rugs to talk things over with those dictators?"

Irene is a great girl and a great actress, but they ought to declare her mouth a lethal weapon. Every moving thing is a target for the blonde murderess.

Everybody came in evening clothes. Except, of course, my pal, Mickey Spane, who is a bum at heart. He would rather be shot out of a cannon at the circus or live in a trailer or pitch a tent in Murrell's Outlet in South Carolina. He hates any of these social events, but his wife, Shari, who is a very talented actress, insisted that the people of the theater would be here and she wanted to come. So, he showed. But in slacks and a torn sport shirt that no respectable sport would be found dead in.

Unlike Barbara Blaze, who was never a professional bitch on dope and is still able to write about it, Mickey is actually Mike Axe who mingles freely with the tough guys and the cops, carries a .45 and could easily kick a girl in the navel if she didn't behave. That is, any girl but his little five-foot wife who calls the shots and he doesn't shoot back!

Mickey found himself a couple of playmates and took over a permanent spot at the corner of the bar. He and his pals made a beautiful quartet. Tony Gomez, the former light-heavyweight champ, came in loaded and stayed that way.

Now he insisted on reciting his favorite soliloquy from *Hamlet*. Who was going to stop him? He still hits pretty good, although he lost his title fourteen years ago after he came out of the Navy and declared he was going to the hospital to get rid of the habit. He did try the night-club circuit and the theater for a while, but the champ who made more comeback attempts than Richard Nixon never really convinced anybody that he could lick anything but a six-cent stamp anymore.

Another member of the Spane foursome was night-club owner Jerry Prentiss, a former civilian who made millions in the shoe business but found it more exciting losing his millions in Broadway shows and night clubs. The last of the group was Tommy Dynamo, who was the silent partner in all of Jerry's enterprises, but not so silent he didn't get the biggest slice. Tommy is the undisputed king of the rackets although his name is never signed to any papers or contracts. He draws no salary from anyplace—but those fringe benefits! You could never believe that Dynamo would harm a fly when you first meet him. His graying temples, his impeccable taste in clothes, and his quiet, soft-spoken manner give him the appearance of a country squire. Only don't cross him or you'll wind up in the country on his special estate—six feet under ground.

The guy doodling at the piano was Hank Talent, a promising young songwriter and TV star until he decided to get high rather than higher up in the business. The death sentence came when he appeared on the Ed Sullivan show completely stoned out of his nut. Luckily for Ed it was at the one o'clock dress rehearsal where his six-minute bit turned into twenty minutes of embarrassing silence. Of course Smiley canceled him for the live performance that night and he hasn't been seen on TV since. Except, maybe, to plug a song on the Joe Franklin show on WOR and even then lovable Joe, who is the last of the young old-timers in the business, personally watches the bad boy for twenty-four hours to keep him on tap until his 10:30 show the next morning.

A late arrival was Alan Murray, who had made a fortune by producing six flop shows in a row. At the moment he was under investigation by Louis Lefkowitz, the Attorney General of the State of New York, for unethical practices in the handling of the angels' monies. But to Alan it was a badge of honor. To him every shot was applause. As long as they spelled his name right. And to boot he was a snotty failure. He was the only man I know who never had a hit and was arrogant on spec. But with each flop he got richer and more antagonistic. In spite of it all every big star tried to attract his attention and the money men pleaded with him to take their loot. All those suckers that are born every minute all found Alan Murray.

Of course I wouldn't have a party without June's mother, Belle Masters, being there. My red-headed mother-in-law is only two years older than me but she tells everybody who will listen that she is two years younger. All you have to do to win her is tell her she looks like June's sister and the house is yours. That is, my house, not hers. Belle is everybody's pal and would give you the shirt off my back if you needed it, and with her around it's very easy to run out of shirts.

Naturally my literary agent, Rose Coleman, showed with B.S. Brooks, the theatrical manager, who is the last of the old-time agents who resents that you get 90 per cent of his money. The B.S. initials in his name do not stand for Bernard Shaw. It was Brooks who booked me on that tour through Southeast Asia where I first fell in love with the Asian people and the Asian culture. It was Brooks who worked it out so that the trip cost me my entire season on television and some of the royalties from my latest book. You see, B.S. is in on all the profits but none of the expenses, which is a good thing for him but like he says, "In order to be a star you got to suffer"—me, not him!

Anyway, my literary agent needed an escort since she will not go out in the dark at night alone and who would bother her when she's with B.S. They'd figure she must be his client and if she is she can't have anything left.

The Fourth Estaters were all over the place. Good guy Marty Bellows, whose column is syndicated in over 400 papers around the world and who remains the same sweet small-town boy who still looks goggle-eyed at the chorus girls from the Copa or the movie star with the 42 bust, was listening to Bill Katz, the reporter from *Stage Light,* the theatrical weekly, spill his venom. Poor Bill watched all the guys around him, like Marty Bellows, make it in the Big Time while he was invited strictly to the second nights. It's tough to be a third-stringer in a business where you are a critic who writes about the big shots but never gets a chance to be one. To say that he was bitter would be the understatement of the year. He made a sour stomach seem like sweet cream. When acid pills got sick they took him. I knew he would louse up the party for the paper, but like it says in the showbusiness oath, "As long as they spell my name right."

Bill had a perfectly logical reason to louse up every one of the people at my party. They were successful and he was a slob. He hated me with a vengeance. At one charity affair I'd introduced all the newspapermen in town—Earl Wilson, Frank Farrell, Leonard Lyons, Hy Gardner, Bert Bacharach, etc., but I didn't see him sitting in the rear of the room at his usual table near the men's room and he never forgave me. He came to all my parties just to keep getting even and I kept inviting this dirty little man just to watch him spill his poison even if I turned out to be one of his victims. It was like standing on the corner watching the scene of an accident.

Down deep I guess I always felt that I couldn't even win him over with good food, fine wine, and important celebrities. After all, that's showbiz. You want a good notice even if it's written on a piece of confetti. We're all alike. We can get 100 good reviews and we never acknowledge them, but one crumb calls you a fourth-rater and we knock our brains out trying to cater to him so we can make him like us. Only you could never win this creep. He was a born loser. I remember once he told me that if he could make one of his targets miss a night's sleep on account of him, he could really enjoy his dinner that night. Nice fellow to bring home to mother only you know the kind of mother I mean.

My favorite guest was Mamie Traum, the judge's wife, who always showed up with her skirts over her knees, about three inches over, patterned stockings and boots. Usually she arrived with a young escort about twenty years her junior. "My husband is on a big case and asked Frank to bring me." But I'm sure the judge didn't ask her to lock herself in the toilet with his messenger. This was her own idea. Very few guests ever saw her, unless, of course, they had a key to the can, which was always locked on the inside. With Mamie holding down the main john for most of the night I was very grateful I had two other bathrooms I could give to my guests.

The party was complete when Sol and Myra Malnick showed with Jack and Mary Dubin. Of course they had several other parties to go to. They haven't missed an opening or an affair since the Boston Tea Party. Myra Malnick is the former Myra Myers, who was a big star on the silent screen and still loves to take bows with all her fans—although it's getting tougher to dig them up all the time.

Jack Dubin is the town's oldest and happiest fan, who

books all his dinner dates and parties through the William Morris office. He's worth millions that he made in the dress business, but he just loves showbusiness celebrities and would rather be with the juggler from the Latin Quarter than the President of Macy's.

When my press agent, Rick Ransom, swished to the center of the room and held up his perfectly manicured hands for silence, you could hear the knives drop. All eyes and ears were suddenly focused on the handsome public relations man who walks lightly but carries a big stick. They knew that he had the ear and typewriter of most of the columns in town . . . so go fool around with Gene Autry. Rick would sell his roommate for a good juicy line that he could feed the newspaper boys, and if he needed material to get a plug for one of his clients you could easily be sacrificed to any one of the column gods that he serviced.

"I offer a toast to our host," he lisped, "the Number One Comic and Good Will Ambassador of our country." All I have to do is take him off the payroll one week and I quickly get off the best-seller list and onto his crap list. "This is the first appearance for Dan Mason since his recent visit with Chiang Kai-shek, Indira Gandhi, and General Nguyen Cao Ky." Naturally he was directing this at the newsboys, particularly Marty Bellows and *Stage Light* reporter Bill Katz. After all, what good is the whole party if we can't get a couple of good items out of it.

I found myself looking for Marty and Bill to see their reaction. It didn't look like it was registering with Bellows. He didn't take his pad and pencil out once. Katz was nowhere in sight. I guessed he just filled himself up with all the poison he could hold and went home to spread the disease.

Always conscious of the newspapermen in the room, Ransom introduced each guest like he'd found a cure for penicillin. "Barbara Blaze—the number one authoress in the

world and the dirtiest." Of course his bitchiness had to show.
"And don't tell us you didn't live the part, Barbara baby—
ha-ha."

"Yes," she threw at him as she took her bow. "But not
with you, sweetie. He was a man."

Everybody took a bow. The newspaper guys as well as
the showpeople. Everybody, that is, except Mamie Traum
who was in the toilet someplace, Bill Katz who had disap-
peared, and Tommy Dynamo who always remains incog-
nito. He is much too shy to get publicity for his business. Any-
how, how would it sound, "Let's give Tommy Dynamo a big
hand. This year alone he killed thirty-two civilians, two mob-
sters and three cops."

"Now, Danny boy," Rick addressed me, "where is the
plaque that was presented to you by the King of Thailand?"

"I'll get it," I said. "It's on the wall in June's john. What
better place for a king's citation than facing the throne?"

"If you see Mamie in there—no regards," he called out
as I left the room.

The door to June's den was shut. I opened the door and
turned on the lights and all I could see was a sea of white.
The floor and the furniture were filled with white powder.
My wife's dressing table was a wreck. The empty powder
boxes were all over the room. It looked like somebody had
left the window open and it snowed into the room only it
was summer and the windows were shut tight.

I tramped through the powder to get to the Powder
Room and that's exactly what it was. Pounds and pounds of
bath powder, talcum powder and face powder were dumped
all over the floor, on top of the rugs, the sink, the bathtub, and
the man who was lying curled up in the corner of the tub. He
was completely covered with powder. He looked like a snow-
man that had been thrown away. He was white from the top
of his head to the bottom of his shoes—except for the streak

of red that was coming out of his chest where the scissors were buried.

I knew at a glance that he was dead. It was the first time I was ever faced with anything like this except on TV or in the movies, but I just knew he was a goner. And I knew it was Bill Katz even though his head was crumpled onto his chest and he was completely covered with powder.

"What the hell do I do now?" I mumbled to myself. Panic started to set in. My heart was beating in rock-and-roll time. "I can't go back into the living room with the plaque as if nothing had happened. I'm a pretty good actor—but a Barrymore I'm not. Oh, my God. Mickey. Mickey Spane. He'll know what to do."

I called my wife on the intercom and asked her not to come in, but to send Mickey into her room and to do it quietly, please, and make sure nobody heard her tell him.

"What's the mystery, Danny boy?" Mickey shouted as he walked into the den. "Where's the murder?"

"Shhh," I warned as I closed the door. "Somebody did get murdered and it's no joke."

"You kidding?" he asked when he saw the look on my face. "Who got killed? Where?"

"Right here in June's bathtub. It's Bill Katz, the reporter for *Stage Light*, the theatrical weekly," I said, shaking as I pointed to the dead body in the tub.

"Who would want to kill him?" Mickey asked.

"Anybody in showbusiness is suspect. Half of New York or Hollywood could have done it. The other half don't know him."

"I mean," he said seriously, "somebody that's here at your party now did it. Obviously he didn't commit suicide."

"No," I said. "He's not that good a critic. Any one of us could have done it, but I never thought it would happen. I expected him to die from an overdose of venom."

"Did you do it?" he asked.

"Of course not," I snapped. "Why would I want to kill him? That's the wrong question. I mean, would I kill a guy in my own house with my own scissors and cover him up with my own wife's powder?"

"That's not what I asked you. All I want to know is, did you do it?"

"No!"

"Now let me ask you a question and I want a straight answer. Are you on anything? Do you use heroin?"

"What the hell kind of a crazy question is that? What do you mean to . . ."

"Just answer me straight. Do you use heroin or peddle it?"

"No. Of course not. I . . ."

"Does June?"

"Certainly not. June is . . ."

"Are you sure?"

"Sure I'm sure. Say, what the hell is this all about? I bring you in because I figure you're my pal. I need you to help me with a dead body that I found in my wife's bathtub and you accuse my wife and me of being addicts or dope peddlers. What are you trying to prove?"

"I'm trying to prove that there is something very odd going on here. This is not just a murder. Somebody obviously has gone through all your wife's powder boxes looking for heroin. Why else would all the powder be on the floor? Whoever it is must be playing for pretty big stakes if he is willing to commit murder to get it. You see, a box of heroin looks like powder and could be put in a powder box and at a glance you couldn't tell the difference. Only a box like that of powder is about three dollars and the same box with heroin is about three million."

"And you think June and I are mixed up in this?"

"Perhaps not with your knowledge. How come your wife has so many different kinds of powder? She's got enough here to open her own drugstore."

"She collects them. She buys them in every country she goes to and all her friends do the same. Not a week passes that somebody doesn't send her a rare box of powder from someplace in the world."

"That's it," Mickey said. "Somebody who knows your wife's hobby probably sent her a box of powder from . . . say . . . Hong Kong . . . and marked it as an undeclared gift under ten dollars. Only instead of powder there was heroin in it. And he came here tonight to collect it."

"Wouldn't he be taking a chance sending three million dollars' worth of merchandise through the mail? And why should he send it to June?"

"It could be the safest way. The customs people very seldom open gifts marked under ten dollars and if they should and they see a box of powder, they would never suspect it could be heroin. They used your wife because she is a legitimate square. Just the kind who might get such a package."

"But," I protested, "how come these characters are so sure that we won't get wise? How do they know it will be so easy for them to collect?"

"Because they must be working with somebody inside your house. Like your maid, for instance."

"Not possible. My maid has been with us for years. She's very loyal."

"Three million dollars could buy a lot of loyalty," Mickey answered. "By the way, where is your maid? I haven't seen her all night."

"She's been home sick. I had to get the caterers to send me an extra girl for the party tonight."

"That's it," Mickey hollered. "She's been sick and she couldn't hand over the box to them so they tried to pick it up personally. Only they didn't get it. Otherwise there wouldn't be such a mess here."

"Do you think Bill Katz was one of them?"

"No, but I do think he followed the murderer into the room just for curiosity and caught him in the act of going through the powder boxes. Katz probably accosted him and the killer had no other alternative. After all, he didn't want his act reviewed in *Stage Light*. It was strictly a case of curiosity killing Katz."

"I don't have enough trouble," I muttered. "You have to make with the jokes. What will we tell the guests?"

"Never mind the guests. What will we tell the police? We'd better call them immediately."

"Do we have to?"

"Of course we have to. What do you want to do with the body? Put it in your scrapbook?"

"You've got to get me out of this, Mick," I pleaded. "You've solved hundreds of other cases in your books. Don't leave me now."

"I love you," he said, "but Shari opens in a new show in California on Friday and I've got to be there or you'll have another dead man on your hands."

"So what?" I begged. "That's four full days away. I've seen you solve three murder cases, a kidnaping, and a double suicide with a rape thrown in within twenty-four hours. And the lights were against you."

"Don't worry, Danny boy," he promised, "I'll do everything I can to get it over with as soon as possible. Now I've got to call the police. So will you go out there like a good little boy and tell your guests the good news and make sure nobody leaves until the police arrive—and I do mean nobody. And get that dame and her lover boy the hell out of the toilet."

Lieutenant Lodge looked more like a Wall Street broker than a homicide officer. His blue-and-white-striped jacket, navy-blue slacks, white-on-white shirt and solid-blue knit tie were right out of the window of Saks Fifth Avenue. If he was awed by the celebrities who surrounded him now, he certainly didn't show it.

Lodge stood in the center of the room where a half-hour before Rick Ransom, my queen press agent, was flying around. The lieutenant spoke very softly. Maybe he didn't sound like all the tough dumb cops I've known from TV and pictures all these years but he sure had everybody's attention.

"Somebody in this room is a killer," he said quietly. "It would be easier on everybody if whoever did it confessed right now. Or if one of you knows anything tell me now. The faster we get this over with the less publicity you all will be mixed up in."

"Is he kidding?" Rick Ransom mumbled to me. "For a front-page story half of these characters would kill their own grandmothers. *Less* publicity? Promise them *more* publicity and they'll confess to anything."

Tommy Dynamo stood up and approached the lieutenant. "I'm Dynamo," he said. "I waited around till you showed so that I could do my duty as a good citizen. I'm here strictly as a guest and I can't afford to get mixed up in any publicity. These hams need it, I don't. So be a good boy and let me scram, huh?"

"How long have you been here?"

"Since ten o'clock. But I never left the bar. If I was to kill this bum, I'd have to do it by remote control."

"That's right," Mickey Spane interrupted. "He was with me all evening. He was never out of my sight."

"And who are you?" the cop asked coldly.

"Are you joshing?" I interjected. "That's Mickey Spane. He's the guy that started Mike Axe. He's solved more crimes than J. Edgar Hoover and he's promised to help us clear this up. He's only got a few days, but if I know the Mick—he'll have it all wrapped up before you finish your report."

"Well, now," Lodge said, "that's very nice of you, Mr. Spane. Only I'd like to offer a little suggestion. This is not television. Or Hollywood. And I'm not collecting material for a book. This is a real live murder and I would really appreciate it if you would stick to playing cops and robbers in your books. I don't know what we'll do without you but we're willing to try. Do I make myself clear, Mr. Spane?"

"Sure, sure," Mickey said. "I don't want any part of it. I just came along for the ride." Turning to me, he said, "Thanks a heap. With friends like you I don't need any enemies."

"Okay," Lodge said to Dynamo, "you can go. Leave your name and address and telephone number with the sergeant and no leaving town unless you inform us, understand?"

"Sure. Thanks. Thanks a lot," Tommy said gratefully. He's the one guy whose business is not helped by publicity. Dynamo ran out of there like a thief. That is, he was out the door as soon as the sergeant took his statement and examined him for traces of powder on his shoes and clothes. There was no use taking his fingerprints. Tommy's are on the honor roll at City Hall. Anyway, there were no fingerprints on the scissors—naturally.

The photographers and coroner stayed busy in June's all-marble powder room while Lodge and the sergeant questioned everybody including Mamie and lover boy, who gave each other an airtight alibi. They swore they never left the guest john next to the kitchen. They said they kept busy reading all the write-ups that I have on the walls of my can. Mamie even quoted some of the reviews on the ceiling.

It was a perfect setting for a murder mystery. My living room is strictly Oriental. With the Chinese faces looking down on us from the paintings on the wall, the Ming, Soong, and Tan figures on the shelves and tables and the Turkish oil lamp, Chinese chandelier, and Oriental rugs it was like a Charlie Chan finale. All the guests were sitting around in a circle and one by one they left to make their statement and get their shoes and clothes examined for powder marks. Of course, anybody who was fast enough to commit this three-million-dollar murder would be smart enough to brush his clothes and clean his shoes before he re-entered the living room.

It was 6 A.M. before everybody vacated my apartment. That is, everybody but Bill Katz. He had left at about 3 A.M. With a little help, of course.

June went over to spend the rest of the night—or what was left of it—with her mother, who was very upset. Mickey was going to stay with me. Shari was taking a plane that morning for Hollywood to finish her last days of rehearsing before her opening on Friday night. It was now Tuesday morning.

"Don't forget," she warned Mick when we drove her to Kennedy airport in my red Cad, "I expect you at my opening. If you have to make like Mike Axe, shoot the broad in the navel, make her confess and get the hell out of here by Friday or you'll have to solve the mystery of the broken marriage."

"Okay, baby." He kissed her. "I can't let this poor soul make it alone. But don't worry. I'll be there by Friday if I have to shoot them all in the navel."

Mickey turned Shari and her luggage over to the porter. Before the plane even took off we were on our way back to the Big Town. "Where does your maid live?" he asked.

"My maid? What do you want with my maid?" I asked.

"I don't like the service in my hotel. What the hell do you think I want her for? I want to find out how she is involved in the case of the spilled powder and the only way to do that is to talk to her and I can't talk to her if you don't tell me where she lives. Now that's not too difficult to understand, is it?"

"I get it. Okay. She lives in a brownstone on East Ninety-fifth Street. I know exactly where it is. I've taken her home a few times when she worked very late."

"How did she come to work for you? Where did you get her? Through an agency or what?"

"No. We met her in Hong Kong in 1961. She was singing in a band at the Peninsula Hotel. I needed a little Chinese doll to give my show a bit of variety. She wasn't too good but she was pretty and she was Oriental. She worked with me all through Southeast Asia. Sort of East meets West. It was good cultural exchange. I told her then if she ever came to New York to look me up.

"About two years ago I got a telephone call from Kim. She'd just arrived in town and could she see me? Naturally I remembered. But I just couldn't get her a job. I asked B.S. Brooks, Rick Ransom, and everybody I knew to try to help. But there just wasn't any work for a pretty little Chinese chick who didn't sing too good."

"But you say she did good in your show over there," Mickey commented.

"Over there! Mixed in with our show. Here they just didn't buy her. Anyway, after a few bad weeks her money ran out. June asked her to stay with us. She started helping June around the house and then eventually we offered to pay her to work on a full-time basis. So, she took the job on the promise that she would stay until she got something in show-business. And what better chance would she have than working in our house where the action is?"

"And in two years—nothing?"

"Oh, she got a club date here and there. Of course we let her out to take it. But nothing really happened although she's still trying."

"Does she know any of your friends personally? I mean, does she see any of them away from your home?" Mick wanted to know.

"Well," I said, "she's friendly with Rick, my fag press agent. He was with me on that tour through Southeast Asia and I know he has been trying to get her some work. And she has been to B.S. Brooks' office on her days off hoping to get booked. I know she went out with the champ a few times, Tony Gomez. You see, she's not just a maid. She's our friend."

"Anybody else?"

"Well . . . oh, yes . . . she worked with Hank Talent on her act. He's a fine piano player and a nice guy. He's come over to the house many times when we're away to rehearse her. In fact, everybody likes her. She's even gotten plugs in the columns. Marty Bellows mentioned her only last Friday with her picture yet—which is more than he's done for me lately."

In less than twenty minutes we were at the 96th Street exit of the FDR Drive. I turned the Cad right on 95th Street and went one and a half blocks west and parked right in front of Kim's building. At 8:25 A.M. there were hardly any cars in the street but dozens of people were walking around.

"What the hell are all these people doing up so early in the morning?" I threw at Mickey as we walked up the steps of the brownstone.

"I know you're not gonna believe it," the Mick answered, "but there are hundreds of people who are up before twelve noon. Some even have to go to work as early as nine A.M."

"Okay, okay," I said. "So I like to sleep late. Getting up before noon is like giving me twenty lashes. Luckily I didn't get to bed yet or I could never be up this early."

We went into the inside hallway and rang the bell to Kim's apartment, 4C. No answer. "She has to be there," I said. "She's been home sick for the past week. If she was okay she'd have been at our house." I tried again. Nothing.

"Maybe the buzzer doesn't work," he said. "Let's see if we can get the superintendent to let us in." We rang the super's bell. We could hear it ringing inside someplace. A minute later a very short, stocky man came out. His head was as bald as a tomato but his mustache could cover two heads. He was wearing dirty brown pants held up by a pair of red suspenders. Nothing else. It was the first time I'd seen a man in suspenders in years.

He peered at us over his black horn-rimmed glasses through the glass door before he opened it. "Vat you vant?" he threw at us. "Ve got no vacancies."

"We want to see Miss Kim Chang," I said. "4C."

"So ring her bell. Vat you bodder me for?"

"She doesn't answer," I explained.

"So she ain't home. So vat you bodder me for?"

"I wanted to pay you the fin I owed you," Mickey said, handing him a five note. "Do you mind if we go upstairs and knock on the door? She's been sick. Maybe she's asleep or maybe her buzzer don't work or something. We're worried about her."

"Oh, sure, sure," he said, pocketing the five-spot. "Please to come in. Come in. Vat you standing out dere for? Come in."

He didn't have to be a superintendent. He could always get a job at Columbia University teaching broken English.

We walked up the four flights of stairs pretty fast. That is, we started fast, but by the time we reached the second floor my tail was really dragging. My lack of sleep and my night training were beginning to show. By the time I reached the fourth floor I needed help to press the button to 4C.

We heard the buzzer loud and clear but nobody answered. Mickey knocked on the door and as he did the door squeaked inward. I pushed the door open slowly and hollered inside, "Hello, Kim? It's me, Dan Mason." No answer. "Kim? Anybody home? Hello? Anybody here?"

The air-conditioner was going full blast and so was the TV set. She couldn't have heard the Beatles hollering with all that going on. I could hear the shower going in the bathroom and the water running in the sink behind the screen that divided the room from her little kitchen. Mickey pulled the screen aside. The coffee was perking like it was ready to explode. Both faucets were going full blast and the flour box was turned upside down. The sink, floor, and shelf were covered with flour.

"Oh, no," I stood there stunned. "Oh, no. Please God not Kim."

Mick wasn't listening. He leaped toward the bathroom and pushed open the door.

The faucets in the sink, tub and shower were all open and the water was gushing out angrily. It was rushing over the tub like the falls, completely flooding the tile floor. With the mixture of powder, it looked like a gray paste was covering the bathroom.

Beautiful little Kim was in the tub face-up. With the empty powder box floating around it looked like a little girl playing with her toys while taking a bath. Only this little girl would never play again. Her eyes were staring straight up and even through the water we could see the ugly marks on her delicate little neck where the son of a bitch had strangled her.

Mickey turned off all the faucets, watching carefully that he didn't obliterate any fingerprints. "The bastard," I yelled, "the dirty bastard. This little doll. How could anybody do anything like this? I'll kill him. I swear. I'll cut his heart out. I'll . . ."

"Will you call the police?" Mickey said quietly. "I know I should leave everything as is but I just can't leave her like this." He lifted her gently out of the tub, like a mother taking her little baby out to dry her, and tenderly laid her on the bed. "We'll have to wait for Lodge," he said. "We can't leave her alone."

"The poor little doll," I kept muttering. "The poor little doll. What good can we do her now? What good is watching her now?"

"We've got to wait for the police. In the first place, the super knows we're here. And anyway, I've got to tell them how we found her. We can't do this alone. We need all the help we can get. And don't sell these boys short. They know the score pretty good."

The two uniformed cops came in first. Only a few minutes after I called. One was a tall, slim, handsome young man who looked liked a West Pointer. The other looked like he was ready for Medicare. As soon as he entered the room he took out his pad and pencil and sat down on the easy chair near the door. "Okay," he said, "your names?"

"I'm Dan Mason," I said.

"The comedian?" he asked.

I nodded. "I'm the one who called. This is Mickey Spane."

"*The* Mickey Spane?"

"None other."

"Say, I've been a great admirer of yours for years.
I got every book you ever wrote," he gushed. "Gee, this is
sure a pleasure. Wait till I tell the missus."

"Which one of you did this?" the West Pointer asked.

"Batman did it," Mickey said sarcastically.

"Oh," the young cop said, "you're one of those wise
guys. Look, mister, I never read your books and I never
heard of you or the comic here. So if you don't want to get
in more trouble than you're already in, just answer the questions. Do I make myself clear?"

"Look here, sonny boy," Mickey fumed, "I was writing
about crime when you weren't even an Eagle Scout. So
have a little respect for your elders. I eat little pipsqueaks like
you for breakfast."

"One more word out of you," the young cop started to
walk toward the Mick, "and I'll . . ."

"Is he giving you any trouble?" Lieutenant Lodge said
from the door.

"I can handle him," the cop said.

"You mean," he said, "that you're not afraid of the
great Mickey Spane? Why, this guy has killed more tough
guys and solved more crimes than J. Edgar Hoover. He's a
one-man army, according to his books anyway."

"Come off it, Lodge," Mickey said. "I came here with
Dan looking for his maid. She's been ill for a week and he
wanted to make sure she was O.K. We found her strangled
in the bathtub. We called you immediately. We could have
gotten the hell out of here, but we waited for you because
we thought we could be of some help. Now get off my back.
And that goes for your toy cop."

"All right," Lodge said, "help."

Mickey told him the whole story. How I met Kim.
How she came to work for me. Everything. Who she went
out with, who she knew personally. Leading up to our own

decision to come visit her after we took Shari to the plane.

"Now," the lieutenant said, "tell me exactly what happened when you got here."

"We rang the downstairs bell. There was no answer. So we asked the super to let us in. When we got up here the door was open and everything was going full blast. The water, TV, radio, percolator, air-conditioner, everything. The kitchen sink was running so I went behind the screen to shut it off. That's when I saw the flour all over the place and I knew he had been here. I rushed to the bathroom and found her lying in the tub."

"Why didn't you leave her there? You know better than to touch anything before the police arrive. You should read your own books."

Mickey ignored the sarcasm. "I just couldn't leave her there. I knew she was dead and everything, but I just couldn't stand seeing her like that. I was careful not to touch anything else and not to smudge any fingerprints."

"Well, now, that was very thoughtful of you. Tell me, *Mister* Spane, have you solved the crime yet? I mean, it's almost nine hours since Bill Katz was murdered. Don't tell me you don't know who the killer is yet? That Mike Axe is sure falling down on the job."

"Go to hell," Mickey said.

"After you," Lodge replied. "Now, I'm warning you. I'm warning both of you. If you know anything that you're not telling me, you're gonna be in big trouble."

"What'll you do?" Mickey asked, "take away our library cards?"

"Look . . ."

"Okay, okay," Mick said. "I want to see this thing over with just as much as you do. More. I've told you all we know. Don't you think we'd like to corner the rat that did this? Don't you think I'd like to get my hands on him?"

"Only keep your hands off. We'll do the handling. Now you're sure you've told me everything you know?"

"Yes, I'm sure," Mickey said. "Except that I think you should be looking for a character that's on the hard stuff. Or at least a fellow traveler. I think you should be talking to the mob. There's a few million bucks mixed up here and that's big business. This couldn't be going on without the mob having their claws on it. The guy that did this is only a stooge—a foil. He's either indebted to the boys for money or they have something on him—or both."

"Well, thanks for everything," Lodge said. "That clears it all up. Now will you both get the hell out of here and keep out of it. Or what happens to you will make Leopold and Loeb look like they were on vacation. Out! Out! Get out! Both of you! And never let me look at you again!"

"I'll make that my life's work," Mickey snapped as the lieutenant slammed the door on us.

"I'm sorry I got you into all this," I said to Mickey when we got into the Cad. "Maybe it's better if you go back to California and forget all about it. I'm sure the cops will clear it all up. I mean, why should you get yourself all loused up with something that really has nothing to do with you."

"Nothing to do with me?" Mickey asked. "Nothing to do with me? You're my pal, aren't you?"

"Sure, but . . ."

"You're in trouble, aren't you?"

"Yes, but . . ."

"But my fanny. If you're in trouble I'm in trouble. Furthermore, I don't like guys who go around strangling little China dolls. If you think I could sit still out there in California while some hophead is going around killing off everybody in showbusiness, you're crazy. Anyway, I hate California and the longer I stay away from there the better. So don't bother me."

"Okay," I said. "I knew that's what you would say. I just wanted to hear you say it. Thanks. Now, where do we go from here?"

"You told me that Kim was friendly with that agent— B.S. something."

"Brooks. And Hank Talent and Rick Ransom and all my friends were her friends. She was more like one of the family than a maid."

"I mean she was closer to some than others. Did you say she went out with Tony Gomez? I mean, on dates?"

"Yes. He took her to dinner on her days off every once in a while. He took her to all the shows and even paid for her lessons at the Dramatic Workshop he attended. Very often they would stay at the house and rehearse the scenes they were given as homework. He was very kind to her. Tony is a good guy even if he is a lousy actor."

"Didn't you know he was on the stuff?"

"Sure I knew but . . ."

"Then why the hell did you let him alone with her?"

"Because I thought he was cured. I even heard him lecture on it. Every paper has carried stories about 'Tony Gomez, the champ who licked the habit.' "

"They never lick it," Mickey said coldly. "At least, I never heard of one who did."

"Well, anyway, he was nice to Kim. That's all I can tell you."

"How nice?" he asked. "Where does he live? Let's go have a talk with him. I have a feeling he knows more than he's telling anybody."

"He's at the Wentworth Towers. But even if he does know something, what makes you think he'll talk to us?"

"To me," Mickey said, "if I can keep him away from the stuff for twenty-four hours. He'll spill his guts to anybody for a fix."

"How can you do that?" I asked.

"Easy. Just promise him a couple of good shots. I'll invite him up to my house in Newburgh. He knows the police are watching him now and it's not too easy to get a fix. So, I sneak him up to my place upstate, chain him to the bed and wait . . ."

"I can't believe Tony would do a thing like that. I just can't believe it."

"I didn't say he did it. But at least we'll be able to eliminate him from the list if we know for sure. For instance, we know you and I didn't do it—right? We were together all morning. Shari couldn't do it. She's on a plane for California. June is with her mother at her house. That leaves them out. Mamie and her lover boy were locked in the toilet all night and Tommy Dynamo never left my sight. By the process of elimination we must find the killer."

"But that can take all year," I protested.

"No, it can't," he muttered. "I've got to be in Los Angeles by Friday. Now, while I'm playing house with Tony, you can do a little leg work for me. Find out if Hank Talent was home this morning. Talk to Alan Murray's secretary. See if Kim ever came to his office. Find out where this B.S. agent and Jerry Prentiss and Rose Coleman and Rick Ransom and all your other guests were this morning. Talk to Barbara Blaze and Irene Gardner. Ask them if they noticed anybody go into the den right before Rick started to make his speech.

"Talk to Marty Bellows. He's always got his nose to the news. Ask him if he smelled anything funny. You can eliminate the two couples who came in late, Myrna Meyers and her husband and that professional party goer. They came in just as Ransom started."

"Okay," I sighed. "You can depend on me. I'll be a regular Sherlock Holmes."

"Now, look, don't let them think, any of them, that you are suspicious of them. Make like it's somebody else we're after. And if you hit upon a clue of any kind—don't—I repeat—don't do anything about it till I get back. Do you understand? Do nothing. Just report to me. Is that clear?"

"Sure, Mick, sure. I'm with you. Anything you say."

When I saw my friend the next day he looked like a fugitive from an oxygen tent. He rang my doorbell at exactly twelve noon. The man who entered my apartment was a shell of the fighting Irishman who had left me about twenty-four hours earlier. His eyes were completely sunken into his head. His lower lip was a symphony of purple, red, and blue and four times the size of his upper lip. His right eye was closed altogether.

"Anybody tell you you look good," I said, "slug 'em."

"I don't feel too good either," he retorted.

"What the hell happened?" I asked.

"You should see the other guy," he grinned.

"What happened?" I repeated. "Did he talk? Did he confess? Tell me, what happened?"

"It worked just like I thought it would. I got him up to my house in Newburgh. I told him to take a little nap while I went out to get the stuff. While he was sleeping, I handcuffed him to the bed. When he got up he was furious. But there was nothing he could do about it. I promised to let him loose as soon as he told me what he knew about the murders. At first he swore he didn't even know Kim was dead.

"As the night wore on and out he started to climb the walls. He promised to kill me and you and Lieutenant Lodge. After a while when the spasms started he was ready to tell anything I wanted to know. By eight o'clock this morning he was on his knees pleading, begging me to let him loose and give him the fix. He swore now he'd be my friend for life if only I'd let him go."

"Well, did he confess?"

"He confessed all right. He confessed to killing Bill Katz and Kim *and* three cops in a cellar in Brooklyn and a couple of stabbings *and* the St. Valentine's Day massacre."

"Well, did he do it or didn't he?"

"How the hell should I know? All I know is that I'm tired. I haven't slept in forty-eight hours. My head feels like it was hit with a sledgehammer."

"What happened?" I asked.

"I was hit with a sledgehammer."

"Did you finally let him go?" I asked.

"Yes, and then he hit me with that sledgehammer he calls a fist."

"But you said he said he would be your friend for life if you let him go."

"So he lied."

"Gee, Mick," I said, "I can't tell you how sorry I am that you got mixed up in this."

"Me too," he answered. "Now if I can only get some sleep."

"Please," I said. "Please use my bed. Take a good hot shower and lie down. I'll look in to see how you are when I get back from the funeral."

"What funeral?"

"Bill Katz. It's at the Riverside at one P.M. I thought I'd look around. You know, the murderer returns to the scene of the crime, etcetera, etcetera."

"Okay," Mickey sighed, "I'll take that shower, put on some fresh clothes and go with you."

"But I thought . . ."

"Never mind what you thought. Get a fresh shirt out of my suitcase and put on some fresh coffee, will you?"

"Sure, Mick, sure. Anything you say."

We took a cab to the chapel. How would it look to drive up to the funeral parlor in a red Cadillac convertible?

On the way over I told Mickey everything I learned while
he was playing catch in Newburgh. Poor Mickey seemed in
a daze. I don't think he heard a word I was saying.

I never saw such a crowd. We had to get out about a
block and a half from the Riverside. "I didn't know this guy
was so popular," Mickey yawned. "This is the biggest funeral
I ever attended. I never saw such a turnout for a heel. How
do you account for it?"

"Just give the public what they want."

"Very funny," he grunted. "You ought to be a comedian or something."

It took us twenty minutes to fight our way through the
crowd. The guy at the door recognized us and let us go into
the chapel. Everybody in showbusiness was there as well
as the hangers-on. Almost all the people who were at my
party were there too and sitting together. It looked like they
all took a bus right from my house.

Barbara Blaze and Rose Coleman were there all dressed
up like it was Saturday night at El Morocco. The hat Irene
Gardner was wearing had to come from her wardrobe in
Naughty Marietta. Mamie Traum was there with the Judge
looking appropriately sad and dignified. There was Marty
Bellows with his pad out recording the celebrities who attended. The Bobbsey Twins Jerry Prentiss and Tommy
Dynamo were sitting together with Alan Murray. Even June
and her mother showed. They were sitting with Rick Ransom in front of Brooks and Talent.

Lieutenant Lodge was standing in back of the last row
overseeing the whole scene like a foreman. Everybody was
there. That is, everybody but Tony Gomez. If he made it,
I hadn't seen him yet.

The Mick and I sat down next to Hank Talent. "What
are you doing here?" I asked him. "I thought you hated him."

"I just wanted to make sure it's true," he answered.

"Did you hear about Kim?" I asked.

"Yeah. Isn't that murder? I mean, who could do a thing like that?"

"By the way," I lied, "I tried to call you yesterday morning to tell you the sad news and you weren't home."

"Oh . . . oh . . ." he hesitated, "I, uh, turned my phone off. I was so tired. By the time I got home it was about six-thirty. I wanted to get some sleep. I had a TV show at noon."

"I saw some of your music in Kim's room," Mickey interjected. "I'm sure the police have it now. Have they talked to you at all?"

"Wh . . why . . w . . . why should they talk to me?" He was really scared.

"Well," Mickey said quietly, "they know you have been seeing her. The superintendent of the building says you are up there all the time. When is the last time you saw her?"

"Gee, I don't know," Hank said. "I mean, I saw her once in a while. I helped her with her act and all. You know. Just friends. I mean . . ." He was shaking as he spoke.

"Look, pal," Mickey whispered, "we're trying to help you. We want to keep you out of this. Now tell me the truth. When is the last time you saw her? Remember, it's better if you tell us than somebody else tells the cops."

"Well," Talent hesitated, "it was—I mean, gee I don't wanna get in trouble. Are you sure it's all right?"

"Sure," Mickey said, "sure. Now when did you see her last?"

"Yesterday morning!" he blurted out.

"Yesterday?" Mickey repeated without any emotion in his voice. "What time was it?"

"About se-se-seven-thirty," he stuttered. "I c-c-couldn't sleep. That Katz murder threw me for a loop. I drove around through the park for a while and then decided to go see Kim. I didn't want to be alone and she's the only one I knew would be up this time of the day. Anyway, I thought of a good bit for her to do in her act."

"How did you know it was seven-thirty?" Mickey asked.

"Well," he began slowly, "I remember I was listening to the radio. I don't remember the program but it was good music and the announcer said in just one minute you'll hear the news at seven-thirty. I was in the park on the east side. I made a right turn on Ninetieth Street, got out of the park and drove over to Kim's house and rang the bell."

"Didn't you call her first to see if she was awake or could receive you?" Mickey asked.

"N-no. I guess I didn't think. I just went there and rang the buzzer."

"Well, what happened? Did she let you right in?" he asked.

"Yes. When I came in the door she was surprised to see me. She said I couldn't stay because she was expecting company. I thought at the time it was odd to have callers so early in the morning but I didn't say anything. I just stayed about five minutes and left."

"That's it?" Mickey said. "Nothing else? Did she offer you a cup of coffee? Anything?"

"No, I swear. That's the whole story. After five minutes I left. My car was parked in front of the house. I got into it and drove straight home, set my alarm for eleven A.M., turned off the phone and went to bed. That's the whole story so help me God."

"So," Mickey said, "you are telling me that when you left Kim she was alive."

"Are you kidding? Of course. I told you I only stayed five minutes."

"Did she tell you who she was expecting?"

"No."

"Did she seem nervous or anxious or anything?" Mickey asked.

"Not that I could see. I was so nervous and embarrassed myself I guess I didn't notice. I mean, she seemed okay. Just wanted me to get the hell out before her caller arrived. I guess when I rang the bell she thought it was he."

"If you know anything more, tell me now," Mickey insisted. "There is still time to save you."

"S-s-save me? What do you mean? I told you the truth. I swear it. I don't know anything else. She was just a kid I was trying to help. I wouldn't have hurt her for anything in the world. A little doll like that."

"Okay," Mickey said. "If you think of anything, call me. I'm staying at Dan's house."

B. S. Brooks leaned over Hank to talk to me. "Hey," he whispered, "you're cracking up. You're murder-happy. You're seeing killers in your dreams."

"Well," I said, "Kim didn't exactly die of old age and believe me that scissor sticking out of Bill Katz's chest was no dream. Maybe you think this funeral is a May party?"

"I mean," B.S. answered, "what the hell's the idea of calling my office to find out if Kim was in to see me and when and calling my home to find out where I was yesterday morning? After all, you're supposed to be my friend."

"Well," I replied quietly, "whoever killed Kim and Bill is supposed to be my friend. After all, only friends were in my home Monday night and one of those friends killed Bill Katz. Now if you didn't do it, you got nothing to worry about. So what the hell are you getting so heated up about?"

"Who's heated up?" he squealed. "Who's heated up? It's just that it's embarrassing in front of my office help to be questioned like that."

"It was more embarrassing to that little doll lying there in that bathtub. Such a sweet innocent little baby," I whispered.

"Innocent?" B.S. hissed. "She wasn't as innocent as you think!"

"What do you mean by that?" I snarled.

"Well, your sweet innocent little doll threatened to tell my wife that I tried to rape her—unless I got her the part in the show that she says I promised her."

"If ever your initials fitted you, B.S., they do right now. Kim wasn't that kind of kid. If I know you, you creep, you tried to sign her on the dotted couch and she refused. A girl would really have to be desperate to lay down for you and Kim wasn't desperate."

"Oh, yeah?" Brooks growled. "Then how come she told me she auditioned on Alan Murray's couch and then he didn't give her the part. Blame him. Not me. I'm only the agent."

"You make me vomit," I said. "By the way, where were you yesterday morning after you left my house? You weren't home. Your wife said you never did get there. She said you phoned that you had to go to some rehearsal. And your secretary said you never showed and she knew nothing about any rehearsal and if there was a rehearsal she would know about it. . . . I don't hear you?"

"Not that it's any of your business, but I was with a friend. It happens she's married and a very respectable gal so I can't tell you her name."

"Oh, come on, B.S.," I spat at him. "That kind of talk went out with the belt in the back and spats. You better produce this girl and it better be legit or you're in big trouble."

"Up yours!" he said with a false bravado. But you could see he didn't mean it. This bum was really worried and it wasn't just about his wife.

The ceremony from the pulpit finally got under way. The eulogies were short and false. One of the editors of *Stage Light* said Katz was a hard worker. Marty Bellows said he knew him for twenty years. Period. And the rabbi talked about his great new life ahead of him. After all, what could they say? That he had clean underwear and a good handwriting? Nobody really listened to the speeches anyway. Everybody showed up just to make sure he was really dead—and they weren't disappointed.

On the way out Mickey bumped into Alan Murray on purpose. "Hey!" he said, slapping him on the back. "I hear you were very friendly with Kim Chang. I hear you were going to put her in your new show. Is that right?"

"Well," he smiled, "I wanted to help the kid but she just didn't fit the part. She just didn't have what it takes."

"You mean," Mickey smiled back, "you just couldn't take what she had."

"What kind of crack is that?" the producer said.

"I heard," Mickey threw at him, "that you tried to audition her on your producer's couch and she refused. Any questions?"

"That's not so," he barked. "You've been talking to that B.S. Brooks. Just because I refused to put any of his whores in my shows he makes up those lies. He's the one who keeps sending me his secondhand merchandise."

"Are you telling me," Mickey asked him, "that Kim was one of his whores?"

"I don't know. All I can tell you is he pleaded with me to get her off his back. He said she'd do anything for a part in my show."

"Well," Mickey prompted, "did she do anything?"

"No. I told you. I'm a legit producer. I wanted to help her but she wasn't right for the part. That's all there was to it."

"When was this that she came up to see you?" Mick asked.

"Oh, about six weeks ago."

"Have you seen her since then?"

"Well, er, here and there, once or twice."

"I mean, let's get specific. If you don't tell it to me you're going to have to tell it to the police."

"Police? What have I got to do with the police?" he barked. "All I did was talk to the girl. I just didn't have a part for her. I'm sorry she's dead and all that but what's that got to do with me—or the police?"

"Look," Mickey began, "you're a friend of Danny's. I'd love to keep you out of it. But you must tell me all you know about her. Did you ever meet her away from your office?"

"Well, yes, once. I took her to dinner. I told you I felt sorry for her."

"The elevator man in your building tells me Kim was up to your apartment several times."

"So what!" he replied. "I'm a bachelor. There's nothing wrong in that. I told you . . ."

"I know, you felt sorry for her. Tell me," Mickey asked, "where were you yesterday morning after you left Danny's apartment?"

"Why . . er . . uh . . I was home. I canceled all my appointments for the morning and went home to bed. You can call my secretary and ask her."

"Why, was your secretary in bed with you?" Mickey asked.

"No, I mean I called her to cancel my appointments. What are you trying to make me say?"

"I'm trying to make you say the truth. Was anybody home with you?"

"No, I told you. I'm a bachelor. I live alone. My maid only works afternoons."

"Well, did anybody see you go into your apartment, like the elevator man or somebody?"

"No," he said. "I don't think so. Our building is self-service from two A.M. until seven A.M. I have a key to the front door and the elevator is self-service. I got home about six-fifteen in the morning and stayed there until I went to rehearsal at two o'clock."

"Very convenient," Mickey muttered.

"I swear it's the truth."

"Danny tells me he called you yesterday morning and you weren't at home," Mickey threw at him.

"Well, I sleep in the rear of the apartment. There is no phone in my bedroom. I was so tired, I guess I just didn't hear it ring."

"Very convenient," Mickey repeated. "It all sounds too phony. First you only met her in your office. Then you took her to dinner. Then you had her up to your apartment. The next thing I'll find out is that she was having your baby."

"No, no, that's not true. I swear," the producer cried. "It was B.S. She tried to blame it on me. She said she was going to tell Marty Bellows that I was the father of her unborn child. She asked me to marry her to give the child a name. How could I? I'm married. My wife lives in Puerto Rico. I haven't seen her in years. But I'm married even though I live like a bachelor. You're the only one who knows this. Please, Mickey, please, keep me out of this. It could ruin me."

"When snakes get drunk," Mickey said to him, "they must see you."

"I swear I told you the truth. You've got to help me, Mickey," Alan pleaded. "Danny, tell him. If ever I needed a friend I need one now."

"If you need a friend, buy a dog," I growled as we walked away and left the big producer standing on the corner of 76th and Amsterdam mumbling to himself.

I hailed a cab and gave him my address. Mick and I didn't say a word to each other the whole way back. The two of us sat there like we just heard the Russians were really coming. When we got out in front of my house Mickey finally said, "Nice friends you got. What jungle did you meet them in? I wanna vomit."

I didn't answer. I just followed him into the elevator. When I got upstairs I found June and her mother were already there. They were sitting in the kitchen with Rick having some tea. Only Rick seemed like he was on some other kind of tea. His eyes were glazed and he was talking in a higher-pitched voice than usual. He was hitting notes that would make Lily Pons sound like a bass.

"The little bitch," he was screeching, "the little bitch. Butter wouldn't melt in her mouth—only poison. Why . . ."

"What little bitch?" I interrupted his opera. "Who are you vivisecting now?"

"Who?" he screeched. "Who? Your precious little China doll Kim Chang, that's who." His voice was so high only dogs could hear him.

"Kim?" I repeated. "Our Kim?"

"I suppose you didn't know she was blackmailing half the town?" he screamed.

"I hope you know what you're saying," Mickey snapped. "If not, you're in big trouble, lady."

"Look here, Mr. Sp . . ."

"And keep your voice down when you talk to me or I'll rip your tongue out of your head. Do you read me right? Now, how do you know Kim was blackmailing anybody?"

"How do I know?" His voice now was at least three octaves lower. "How do I know? If Dan was paying her fifty dollars a week, how come she was sending home to mamma three hundred a week—huh? And I should know. I'm the one who made out the money orders for her."

"So if you knew this, how come you didn't tell Dan or June about it? After all, you're supposed to be their drum beater and friend. How come you kept this such a secret until now when she can't answer you?"

"Because I was one of her victims, that's why. She promised to go to the police if I as much as breathed a word to anybody."

"What did she have on you that made you the fink of the year?" Mickey asked.

"That died with her," he said.

"Yeah," Mickey spat at him, "so *you* did the double killing."

"No, no. I swear. I had nothing to do with it. I'm glad she's dead. I'm glad, do you hear? But I had nothing to do with it." He sounded like a hysterical chorus girl. "I hated her, hated her. But I could never touch her. I couldn't harm a fly," he cried.

"Not unless it was open," Mickey said disgustedly. "Who was she blackmailing, besides you?"

"I can't tell you that. It's not fair," he squealed. "Why make trouble for these people? Let their secrets be buried with her. They suffered enough."

"If you think *they* suffered," Mickey threatened, "when I get through with you, you'll wish you were with Kim now. I want to know everybody you say she blackmailed. I want to know everything you know and I want to know it now. Do you hear me?"

"Sure, Mickey, sure." He was scared stiff. "Sure, but please don't get me all mixed up in this. Please. I don't want any more trouble."

"It'll die with us," Mickey assured him. "Now names, please."

"Well," he hesitated, "she learned that Irene Gardner had her face and bust lifted three times. She found out who the doctor was and threatened to tell the story to *Private* magazine unless she was put on the payroll."

"But," June interrupted, "we all knew Irene had a lift job. What's the big secret?"

"Sure," Rick admitted, "but only a Kim Chang would use it. And she had Before and After pictures to prove it. *Private* would sell their editor to get their hands on those photos and Irene knew it."

"Who else?" Mickey asked.

"She told B.S. and Alan Murray they were the father of her unborn child which she wasn't having. She threatened Tony Gomez she would tell Marty Bellows he was back on the hard stuff. She swore to Jerry Prentiss she would tell the license bureau that Tommy Dynamo really owned the club and the discotheque. Jerry's name is on the license, but she had proof that Tommy owns them lock, stock, and twisters. She told Mamie she'd go to the judge about her toilet habits. She even got in the act with Rose Coleman. One of her clients is a disk jockey, Ronnie Davis, who wrote a couple of books. Well, the China doll had proof that he was on the take. Payola. All of them paid rather than chance the bad publicity."

"If what he says is true," Mickey said to June and me, "you really inherited a beaut. What hole did you dig her out of?"

June was in tears. "I don't believe it. It couldn't be true. She wasn't that kind of a girl."

"She wasn't, huh?" Rick was riding now. "Well, I didn't want to tell you . . . but she had pictures of you when you posed in the nude for that photographer when you first came around this town. Remember?"

"But," June looked at me, "I thought those things were destroyed years ago. How . . . ?"

"Easy," Rick said. "Sure, Dan and I went to see this bum after you were married. He swore he gave us every picture *and* the negatives. But you know you can't trust those rats. He just kept another set of negatives, I guess, and Kim found them."

"But," I interrupted, "how come she never blackmailed us? How come she never said a thing to June or me?"

"Because," he explained, "she needed a base of operation and you were it. She wouldn't use it on you unless she had to. Or she was ready to make her exit."

"If you knew all this," Mickey looked at him like he just crawled out from under a rock, "then why didn't you tell Dan or June about it? Don't you think you owe them something? Don't you know it's against the law to withhold evidence like this? You can go to jail for life. An accessory after the fact. If they get you, they'll throw away the key."

"But I told you," he whimpered, "she had me tied up in knots. She could have ruined me."

"You fink," Mickey said between his teeth. "Get the hell out of here before I really ruin you."

"Remember," Ransom whined as he stood up, "you promised you wouldn't tell this to anybody. You gave your word."

"If you're not out that door in two seconds," Mickey hollered, "you'll go out the window."

He made it in the time allotted him.

June's mother spoke for the first time. "Drop it. Drop the whole thing," she demanded. "Before we all get killed."

"But, Belle," I said, "we're mixed up in this thing whether we like it or not. We can't just walk out now."

"Well," she spat, "I don't like it. If you don't walk out now you'll be carried out. Aren't two murders enough for you? What are you trying to do—try for three? You're the only family I have. I don't want any dead heroes in my family."

She started to cry. "Let the police handle it, I beg of you. They know what they're doing. And they're paid for it.

Let them handle it. But please, please, stay out of it. Please
—please . . ."

June put her arms around her. "Mom," she said, "don't
cry. We'll be all right. Don't worry."

"I'm sorry, Mrs. Masters," Mickey said, trying to soothe
her. "I want to be in this less than you do. Shari is waiting
for me in California. If I'm not there the day after tomorrow
you may have to take in a boarder. Come to think of it, that
might be a good idea. You and me could be a hell of a thing."

"What would she do with an old man like you?" I interrupted. "She's got a handsome young son-in-law living with
her now."

"Young?" June hollered. "Young? In a couple of years
when you go to the Old Age home, you and Mick will go as
a package deal."

Mom was smiling now as she wiped her eyes and blew
her nose. "Don't think you're fooling me one bit," she said.
"I'm sorry. These last few days have upset me terribly."

"Don't you see, Mom," Mickey said, "we can't run away
from this now even if we wanted to. As long as that heroin
is missing, we're all in danger. And obviously they haven't
found it yet or they wouldn't be on this rampage. Even if we
pulled out, they'd find us. No matter where we went. These
boys have several million reasons for being in this and they're
all greenbacks. And you know these boys play for keeps.
You've seen some of their handiwork in the last few days."

"Well, what do we do?" Mrs. Masters asked. "Just make
like guinea pigs and wait around to be slaughtered?"

"Exactly," Mickey said, "only I'm gonna be the guinea
pig. And I'm not waiting around. It's about time we brought
the fight to them."

"What do you mean?" June asked.

"Look," Mickey explained, "we got more suspects than
they got in Sing Sing. The guy or gal who committed these

murders is just a stooge—an errand boy. He's expendable. The big babies are the ones I'm after. The ones that give the orders. And I've got to go to them. It's the only way to stop these killings, and clean this up. Then we can all go home and get some love."

"How are you going to do all this?" June insisted.

"If I don't tell you, you're better off. What you don't know can't hurt you. The first thing I gotta do is get out of here and check into a hotel."

"But why?" she asked. "Aren't you comfortable here?"

"Sure," he said, "but I want to get them off your back. Mamma's right. If I'm to be the guinea pig, I don't want the other little piggies to get hurt during the experiment."

I knew I couldn't argue with the Mick. Once he made up his mind, all I could do was follow. I helped him pack. That is, I put his suit and toothbrush in his suitcase. Two pairs of his socks and an old shirt were already lying there —dead to the world.

I insisted on driving him over to the Terrace Hotel in the Cad. After all, how would it look to send my own special guinea pig to the laboratory in a taxi? Anyway, I wanted to know what he was up to. I knew he wouldn't talk in front of the gals.

"What's your plan?" I asked when we got in the car.

"I have no specific plan—I'm gonna have to play it by ear. All I know is, I've got to set myself up as a target—and fast. I'm gonna drop the word in all the wrong circles that I got the stuff and I'm ready to make a deal. Somewhere along the crooked line I'll get to the dirty bottom of this."

"I don't like it," I said. "When they find out you haven't got it, they ain't gonna like it—or you. And when they don't like somebody, they get rid of him. You're too big a target to miss. No, Mickey, I can't let you do it."

"But you will," he said. "I haven't got the time to see

every suspect and beat the truth out of him. Anyway, I'd
be accused of civilian brutality. Believe me, Danny boy, it's
the only way. Now will you do me a big favor and let me get
some sleep? I haven't been to bed since Sunday night. It's
now six P.M. Wednesday and I still got a few calls to make
before I can get some shut-eye. Listen, even guinea pigs
need some rest if they expect a faster reaction."

"Bye, Mick," I said as I pulled up to the Terrace Hotel.
"I'll never forget you for this. How can I ever thank you?"

"If you see Lieutenant Lodge," he said, "no regards."
He grabbed his bag and rushed through the revolving doors
and was gone before I had a chance to really tell him how
I felt. I hadn't had more than two or three hours' sleep since
this whole nightmare started a hundred years ago. Was it
only two days since we found Bill in my wife's bathtub?

I went home to try to get some rest myself. I was never
so tired in my life. I was dead. I needed sleep so badly, but
it was impossible, and I tossed around for a couple of hours
and then decided it was no use. I got up, took a shower,
put on a pair of slacks and a sport shirt and went into the
kitchen to make myself some good hot coffee. If I was going
to be awake, I might as well be wide awake.

"How did it all start?" I thought as I sipped on the
black coffee. Why me? Just because my wife collects powder? Is that any reason for me to collect dead bodies? How
could I have been such a jerk about Kim? And Rick. He's
supposed to be my friend. I gave him his first job as a press
agent. How could he let her do this to me and my friends
and not tell me? How could he let her use me like this? And
that B.S. and Murray. How did I ever collect such friends?
What did I ever do to win Tony Gomez? And Hank Talent?
Poor Irene Gardner. She has to have her face and bust lifted
every season and then she's got to pay off to keep it from
getting into print. Poor soul. Doesn't she know that every-

body knows about it anyway? I wonder would she kill to keep the worst-kept secret in town? How about Hank, B.S., Alan, or Tony? Are they capable of murder? Any of them? How about the Fag? Could he have done it? Or Tommy Dynamo? He wouldn't have to do it himself. All he has to do is nod and you're dead. Could it be that disk jockey or Rose Coleman? She'd do anything for a client. I remember she once threatened to kill that Frank Ryan from the *Globe* because he said one of her writers, Sam Dorman, couldn't write a laundry list without help. Jerry Prentiss maybe? He's a rough guy when he's crossed. Who? Who would use my wife's bathtub as a garbage dump?

Somewhere a bell was ringing. It kept coming closer and closer. Louder and louder. "The alarm clock," I thought. "Why doesn't it stop? It's an eight-day ring. Somebody has got to turn it off or it'll wake the whole world. Poor Mickey, he needs the sleep. I've got to stop that clock." I stretched out my hand to shut it off and dumped the cold coffee in my lap. I jumped up like I was shot out of a cannon. I must have dozed off. The bell was still ringing. It was the phone. I picked it up.

"Where the hell is this phone—in the candy store?" It was Mickey.

"I'm sorry," I said drowsily, "I didn't hear it."

"What do you want—chimes? Next time I'll send up flares. I've been trying to get you for the last ten minutes. Where the hell have you been?"

"Here," I answered. "I guess I dozed off. What time is it?"

"It's eight-thirty," he said.

"What kind of eight-thirty?" I asked sleepily.

"What kind would you like, chocolate or vanilla?"

"I mean," I said, "eight-thirty at night?"

"It's eight-thirty in the morning, you idiot," he barked.

"Now will you get yourself together and get over here right away? I got a job for you. I'm in room 12C."

"Eight-thirty in the morning!" I jumped. "Holy mackerel. I slept on the kitchen table all night. I really must have been tired. Holy mackerel. Eight-thirty in the morning!"

"Look, Rip Van Winkle," he started quietly, "when you wake up, will you drop over and see me? Do you think you can make it in twenty or thirty years? What do you say, Rip?" Now he was yelling like he was on fire.

"I'm sorry, Mick," I said, "I'm up now. I'll be over in a few minutes. I'm sorry. What room are you in again?"

"12C," he said, "and hurry it up." He slammed the receiver down.

When Mickey opened the door for me, I thought I was in the wrong room. I never saw a face like that in my life. He looked like he went 15 rounds with Mohammed Ali. Either that or he called the witch doctor a jerk. His face had more colors and lumps than a pinball machine. He sure looked like he was tilted, too.

"Say," I said, "it's a little early for Halloween, isn't it? What's with the mask, pal?"

"Very funny!" he hissed between bruised lips. "How come you don't get such laughs in your act?"

"Don't you ever win?" I asked. "In your books, it's always the other guy that gets the lumps."

"I guess these bums don't read my books," he grinned. "I'll tell you one thing—fans they're not."

"Why, Mickey?" I asked seriously. "Why did they do it?"

"I guess they just don't like me," he smiled.

"No," I said, "I mean what happened?"

"Nothing much," Mickey said. "Like I said, I dropped the word that I had the stuff. Naturally they came looking for it and me. They called my bluff. I tried to make a deal with them but they had the cards stacked. You can't beat a full house—and this house was full of hoods with all kinds of pat hands fitted with brass knuckles, saps, and guns."

Now I noticed the room for the first time. It looked like an indoor hurricane had hit it. The chairs and sofa were cut wide open with their guts hanging out. All the dresser drawers were dumped on the floor upside down. The mattress on the bed was a mass of wounds with its insides spilled all over the floor. Mickey's suit was ripped apart. Even his shoes were torn and the heels ripped off.

"It looks like they did a pretty thorough job," I said. "Did they find anything?"

"What was there for them to find—my old socks? Lucky for me I don't have it or I'd be dead. These are pros. They don't want me. They want the stuff. It's millions for them. They figure if I got it stashed someplace, they have to keep me alive till they find it or convince me to hand it over. And believe me, these hoods present a pretty strong case."

"Enough is too much," I said. "I got you into this and now I'm getting you out of it. We're going to the police. I can't let you sacrifice yourself anymore. You could get killed. I'd never forgive myself."

"I wouldn't like it too much myself," he laughed.

"No, I mean it," I insisted, "we're going to the police."

"We're going no place," Mickey said, "except to your apartment. That's what I wanted to see you about. I know the killer now. I'd like to wrap him up and deliver him tonight. Now, call everybody who was in your home Monday night and get them there tonight. Make sure they all show, if you have to threaten, drag, or kidnap them. Only get them there. That's your job. Nine o'clock tonight. *I'll* personally see that Lodge gets there."

"Don't worry," I said, "I'll get them there if I have to

bind and gag each one personally. Who's the killer, Mick? Who's the rat that started this revolution?"

"You'll find out tonight," he said quietly, "and don't worry. The revolution is over. You'll have plenty of shouting tonight. Now do me a favor and ask the bellhop to come up here. I need some clothes for tonight. These bums ruined my wardrobe—and will you get Lieutenant Lodge on the phone for me, while I try to patch up this kisser of mine."

"Leave it alone," I said, "it's an improvement. You never looked better."

"Yeah, I know," he said. "I'm really a wreck. You should see my body!"

"Is that an offer?" I ribbed.

"Are you kidding?" he laughed. "Even if I switched you wouldn't be first."

When I got Lodge I handed the phone to Mickey. "How are you, Lieutenant?" he said lovingly. "I miss you." All I could hear was loud squawking coming out of the receiver. "Look, Lieutenant," he continued, "one more crack like that and I'll report you to the Civilian Review Board for Police Brutality."

The receiver almost exploded. "Now calm down," Mickey tried to soothe him. "Meet me at Mason's apartment at nine tonight. The whole cast will be there and I promise to deliver the star—all gift-wrapped." More squawks. "Look," he said, "what have you got to lose? I don't deliver, you always got me." The squawking was louder now. "Okay," Mickey said, "then I'll see you at nine—and the same to you!"

"Is he coming?" I asked when he hung up.

"He'll be there," he said, "if he ever comes down off the ceiling."

"Come in, it's open," I hollered in response to a persistent knocking on the door. The bellhop walked into the room followed by the biggest blonde I ever saw. She was about six feet tall and stacked with gold—and none of the jewels were hidden. The white satin gown was cut down to her air-conditioning, revealing a treasure chest that made Sophia Loren look like a boy.

Mickey ignored her completely, like she wasn't even in the room. "Have these shoes fixed," he said to the bellhop. "Somebody ripped the heels off. And have the tailor clean the blood off this suit, fix the lining and pockets and press it." With that he took off the suit he was wearing and handed it to the boy, leaving him standing there in his shorts, socks, and bloody shirt. "And get me a pair of socks, size ten and a half, and a white shirt —17, 33 sleeve—okay? Got it all? I need everything by eight o'clock tonight."

"I got you, Mr. Spane," the boy said as he continued writing. "You can depend on me. You're my favorite writer in the whole world. Boy, how you take care of these tough guys. You're my man."

"Thanks, pal," Mickey said. "Now don't forget, I need it all back by eight o'clock tonight."

"Sure," he said, "don't worry about a thing. Hey! What happened to your face?"

"Oh, nothing," Mickey said. "I ran into an army."

"I'd hate to see that army now," the boy said admiringly as he shut the door behind him.

"Is there any little thing *I* can do for you?" the blonde cooed as she sashayed toward Mickey with all her jets open.

"No, thanks," he smiled. "It's as much as I can handle for one day."

"You mean," she said, "you can't take it?"

"I mean," he said, "I'm going to take it with me—to California—tonight!"

"You mean," she said, "you don't wanna play?"

"I mean," he said, "I'm a broken umbrella. I hurt all over."

She put her arms around him and kissed him on the neck. "Now," she cooed, "that doesn't hurt, does it?"

"Only when I love," he said as he shoved her away with a vicious slap on the derriere.

"You see?" he looked at me. "And Shari thinks I'm enjoying myself."

"I hate to tear myself away from you two," I said. "I know you're gonna miss me. But I got a lot of rounding up to do. See you tonight at nine, Mick—and remember, Shari hits like a heavyweight."

"What the hell," he said. "A job is a job."

"How come a thing like this never happens to me?" I asked with my hand on the doorknob. "I'm better looking than you, and besides, I get more laughs."

"Can I help it if my readers are faithful?" he smiled. "They believe me."

"Nobody can ever tell me again you don't live the part," I said. "Don't misunderstand, I don't envy you. I just want to do your research. Good day, Mr. Spane."

The scene in my apartment looked like a rerun. It was as if we taped the show and replayed it live. The cast and characters were the same as Monday night. Only three days ago, but it seemed like three years. I even arranged the same caterers and insisted they send the same help. The only one of the original party that was missing was Bill Katz. And we weren't going to dig him up just to please my friend Mickey Spane.

The only added starters were the two extra "waiters" that arrived with Lieutenant Lodge about fifteen minutes before post time. Believe me, I felt much better when I opened the door for them at 8:45. Mickey showed a few minutes later in a very serious mood. He looked ready.

"I'm giving you enough rope," Lodge greeted him. "If you don't tie up the killer, you can always hang yourself," he said sarcastically.

Mickey wasn't having any of it. "Look," he growled, "if you want to make with the jokes, throw your own party. I don't want to butt into your job. I'm in this because a pal of mine is involved and he asked me to help. I'd like to see this cleared up as soon as possible so I can get the hell out of your town and go back to my wife in California."

"Nothing would give me greater pleasure," Lodge answered smugly.

"You ought to give lectures on 'How To Lose Friends And Influence Nobody,'" Mickey threw back. "You could make Emily Post and Dale Carnegie . . ." The doorbell rang loud and clear.

"Saved by the bell," I hollered. "You two are the greatest since Smith and Dale. Why don't you go on the stage? When this is all over, I'm going to talk to B.S. and get him to line up a tour for you two."

"And B.S. to you, too," Mickey said as he walked into the den.

Tony Gomez arrived with Jerry Prentiss and, of course, Tommy Dynamo. B.S. and Rose Coleman came together like they did the night of the murder. Alan Murray arrived alone. As did Marty Bellows. The Malnicks and the Dubins came as a package deal. Rick Ransom, Barbara Blaze, and Irene Gardner entered together. They met in the lobby and made the trip up in the elevator as a trio. Hank Talent strolled in by himself. Mamie Traum and her lover boy were the last to make the scene.

By 9:20 the whole cast was there. When everybody had a drink in his hand Mickey entered stage left with June and her mother on either side of him like bookends. The girls took their seats. The stage was set. Mickey stepped front and center to open the show.

"Somebody in this room is a killer," he started. How's that for an opening line? "And," he continued, "I know now who it is." Everybody looked around at each other like they were sitting next to a leper. Even June and her mother took a few hard stares. Bellows squirmed in his seat. Lieutenant Lodge standing in the doorway was watching all the faces. Looking for some reaction. One false move.

"This was murder for profit," Mickey continued. "Whoever committed these killings did them strictly for cash. It was a labor of hate. 'Anybody who interferes with my making a living has got to go.' You know, nothing personal.

"Let me set the scene for you. The plot is very simple. There is about three million dollars' worth of heroin involved here that belongs to the mob. That is, they expect to get that much out of it in the market.

"It all started when one of their lay executives sent a box of powder probably from Hong Kong. It was for Mason's wife, who is a well-known collector of different powders. Only instead of powder they filled the box with heroin. They figured if they sent it as a gift parcel under ten dollars, nobody would notice. And if customs opened the package and saw the box of powder they would never think anything. Especially if it was going to June Mason, a known personality and world traveler. Most likely they had even read about her famous collection of powders.

"Of course they needed somebody in the Mason home to pick up their precious cargo. They knew June or Dan or her mother wouldn't be any part of it. But they didn't need them. They had their own built-in receiver—Kim Chang, the Mason maid. She was a perfect pigeon for the mob—a hungry dame with ambitions who would do anything to turn a dishonest buck.

"But something went wrong. When the fink who was the contact between the pigeon and the mob asked her to hand over the powder, she reneged. I don't know if she wanted a bigger slice of the take, or if she didn't want to do anything that would spoil her base of operations. Or maybe she just got religion and didn't want to implicate the Masons, who had been so good to her.

"Most likely she just got scared. Being a front woman for Mr. Fink's blackmail business with a bunch of scared showpeople is one thing, but dope and mobs . . .

"Anyway, she didn't want any part of it. She took suddenly sick, very conveniently, and stayed away from the Mason home. When the fink couldn't convince Kim by pleas, promises, or threats, he decided to get the stuff himself. He knew the boys don't accept failure. Especially a three-million-dollar flop.

"And remember this was *his* idea. *His* baby. He had Kim all sewed up, he told the boss. So, he had to deliver or it was *his* funeral.

"You all know what happened at the party. He committed murder to get the powder. Only he didn't get it. The only thing he could conjure up in his evil brain was a double-cross by his erstwhile associate, Kim Chang. He was desperate. When he was released by the police Tuesday morning he called her. He had to see her right away. That must have been about six-thirty or seven in the morning. She told him to give her an hour or so. He arrived at about seven-thirty."

"I told you," Hank Talent screamed. "I told you I went to see her at seven-thirty—but I only stayed five minutes. I had nothing to do with all this—I told you—you promised to keep me out of it."

"I didn't mention your name, did I? But now that you bring it up," Mickey said, "do you mind if I ask you a question? Do you always go calling on girls at seven-thirty in the morning?"

"But she wasn't just a girl. She was *my* girl. I was in love with her. We were going to be married. I wouldn't hurt Kim. I loved her. I loved her . . ."

"Why, you small-time piano player." It was Tony Gomez. "She wouldn't have married you if you could buy her Broadway. She was only using you to help her with her act. You knew she was my girl, you chiseler. You killed her . . . you killed her. . . . Why, you dirty. . . ." The two "waiters" held him in his seat.

"I didn't do it, I swear," Hank cried. "You've got to believe me. I . . ."

"I believe you," Mickey said quietly. "You parked your car in front of her house at seven-thirty. You see, Tony, if he was going to kill her, he certainly wouldn't advertise it. Dozens of people are walking around at seven-thirty in the morning on East 95th Street. One of them had to spot the car and report it to the police if a murder was committed. It would be like putting up a neon sign.

"The real killer was smarter than that. He parked his car around the corner. Or maybe he came by taxi and got off a couple of blocks away. Anyway, when he saw your car in front of the house he waited for you to come out and then went up to do his job."

"It was Gomez," Hank hollered. "He did it. He was jealous of me. She must have been his partner. Why else would she go with a gorilla like that? Poor Kim. She'd do anything to become a star and she thought she could do it by getting money enough to buy her way."

"Why, you dirty little punk," Gomez yelled and started to get up.

"Don't force us to tie you up," the waiter said. "Sit still or you'll lie still."

"What makes you think Tony is involved in this?" Mickey asked Hank.

"Everybody knows he's still on the stuff. No matter what he says in the papers. Where is he getting his loot? Dope is a pretty expensive habit. I know Kim was in on something that wasn't kosher. She always flashed a big bank roll. He must have been the contact. He was a perfect stooge for the mob— an ex-pug who was hooked.

"She swore to me she would quit as soon as she got enough to get herself a show. Then we could get married. She told me she was on to something real big and we could expect a wedding any day now. She must have told Gomez. He figured she grabbed the stuff for herself and he killed her. The lousy junky killed my girl."

Gomez sat there a broken man. All the fight was out of him. "I never touched her," he mumbled. "She was my girl. I paid for her dramatic school, we rehearsed scenes together. Why would I hurt her? She was the only thing in my life."

"Tell me, Champ," Mickey asked, "where do you get your money? You haven't fought in three years and you certainly aren't making any fortunes on the stage."

"Not that it's any business of yours," Gomez mumbled, "but my manager, Irving Goldman, God love him, arranged an annuity for me years ago. He made it so I couldn't touch the capital. I get a good lump every week for the rest of my life. He's a great guy, that Goldman. And he isn't in the racket. I didn't get mixed up with mob guys then and I don't now."

"That's right," I interrupted. "I called Goldman while you were in Newburgh, Mickey, and he told me the exact same story. Goldman is a very successful lawyer. He would have no reason to lie."

"I know," Mickey said. "Tony would have no reason to kill her. The killer was trying to protect his own life. He was in business with her . . ."

"Why don't you ask Mr. B.S. Brooks about his business with her?" Rick Ransom canaried.

"What kind of business?" Mickey asked.

"What other kind of business does Brooks handle but whores?" he answered. "He promised her the world. He said he would get her the lead in a Broadway show. All she had to do was lay down and talk it over. Then he handed her over to Alan Murray, who gave her his personal audition."

"That's a lie," Alan Murray shouted. "And you know it."

"This kid was so ambitious," Rick continued, ignoring the producer, "she would do anything for a part. She was so desperate, she even did it with Brooks and Murray."

"Don't get me mixed up in this," Murray shouted. "She was Brooks' merchandise. It was his baby she was having—not mine. He promised her a show—not me. When she threatened to tell his wife he got panicky."

"And killed her?" Mickey asked.

"Why, you small-time hustler," B.S. shouted at Murray. "How could you lie like that? You were the one who made all the promises to her. It was your baby she was having."

"That's a lie," Murray screamed.

"Yeah," B.S. continued, "then how come you were paying her off every week—and plenty."

"I was just trying to help the kid till . . ."

"You wouldn't help your grandmother if she were starving," B.S. snarled.

"Now this is what I call a cozy little party," Mickey finally interrupted. "Almost any one of you could have killed her. She was blackmailing practically everybody in this room except the fink who did it. He was her partner.

"The fact is, Kim was only the foil—the stooge. Our fink was the head errand boy for the mob. She didn't even know anything about the mob. She just took her orders from him. He is the one who discovered everybody's weakness and then turned it over to her to blackmail them. Naturally, he wouldn't show himself. That's why it was so tough to grab him.

"I knew the only way was to go to the mob. Kim couldn't talk and naturally he wouldn't. So I decided to go to the source.

"I figured if I dropped a hint that I had the stuff they would be willing to make a deal. I know these punks pretty good. For three million they would sacrifice their mother— all I wanted was the killer.

"When I dropped the word, it reached the right ears in a matter of minutes. Naturally they called in their leg man— our own fink. They weren't going to liquidate him until they had the stuff. So they sent him to see me with a squad of goons.

"Of course, he waited on the corner. He didn't want to reveal himself unless it was to kill me. His orders were to keep me alive till I turned over the merchandise. First they offered me money. Then they offered me lumps—and they did a pretty good job on me. You know, I wasn't born with this face.

"When this didn't work, they sent me the biggest bust in town. A typical Mike Axe blonde. She offered me everything but the killer—and that's the only thing I wanted. No killer —no trade. The fact that I didn't have anything to trade with —this they didn't know. Which is what kept me alive.

"When she failed with her body, she finally offered her trump card. 'It happens that I got some nude pictures of a friend of yours,' she purred. 'I'd much rather give them to you than the magazines. You can have them with the negatives—guaranteed—for the package. The stuff can't do you any good anyway. You can't peddle it. In addition, we will give you fifty thousand in cash. Fifty grand. What do you say?"

"I got so excited I kissed her on the lips and threw her the hell out of the room. She didn't know it, but she had just told me who the killer was.

"Rick Ransom," Mickey spat out, "you are the only one who knew about those pictures besides her husband and me. Remember? You're the one who made the deal with that fink photographer!"

"Me?" Rick squealed. "Me? Kim is the one who had the pictures. I told you she had them."

"You told me that she had something on everybody in this room and many more. You also told me that the reason you didn't expose her is that she had something on you and was blackmailing you, too."

"That's true," he sobbed.

"The truth is," Mickey continued, "it was the other way around. *You* had something on *her*. You knew she was blackmailing Brooks and Murray—telling them she was having their baby. You also knew that she wasn't going to have anybody's baby. That was all part of the lie to get her in a Broadway show."

"How do you like that? Why, the dirty little fraud," B.S. hissed.

"How could I have been such a jerk?" Murray mumbled. "And I paid her a fortune because I thought she was pregnant. I felt sorry for her."

"Ransom," Mickey continued, "a little girl like Kim Chang, fresh from Hong Kong, couldn't possibly know all the scandal in this town. Dan didn't know. I didn't. How would she know if a star had her face lifted, and have pictures to prove it? How would she know what racket guy owned a piece of what club? What would she know about Payola and dope and mobs?"

Mickey pointed his finger at him. "You told her, Rick. You put her in business. First you probably threatened to tell Brooks and Murray that the baby stuff was a phony. Then you told her to ask them for money. If she was going to play the game, she might as well share in the profits.

"You found out about the skeletons in all the closets. Then you used her as the bait, the front woman, the stooge. She collected while you sat in the background and set up all the plays."

"Then why would I kill her?" Rick asked defiantly.

"Because," Mickey answered, "you were on the spot. The mob was hounding you for the package. You had already killed one man to get it and failed. And you thought she had double-crossed you and kept the stuff for herself.

"Furthermore, you knew that when she heard about the murder and the powder, she would realize immediately that you and you alone had done it. And you didn't want any witnesses pointing their finger at you.

"So, when you left this house Tuesday morning, you called Kim. After all, you were in business together. You knew she would see you. When you got to the house you saw Hank Talent's convertible sitting at the curb. You recognized it immediately. Hank is your client. You've been in his car dozens of times. So, you waited on the corner for him to come out and drive away.

"Then you opened the front door with the key she gave you. After all, you're her partner. And I'm sure you kept all the files up there. What safer place than little Kim's apartment? Naturally, you had to have a key for the files. Suppose you needed some blackjack material in a hurry and Kim wasn't there?

"Anyway, what did Kim have to worry about? She knew you wouldn't attack her. She wasn't your type. She was a girl.

"But she never figured on murder. When you got up to

her apartment she didn't suspect a thing. She put the coffee on and sat down to wait for orders.

"Instead you accused her of grabbing the package and stashing it. You ripped her apartment apart trying to find it. All the flour and powder all over the house. When you were convinced she knew nothing about it, you strangled her anyway just to make sure she didn't talk."

"But," Rick snickered, "you said the alleged murderer killed Kim *and* Bill Katz. Now why would I kill a guy like Katz? What did he have to do with it?"

"That was strictly an accident," Mickey answered. "Big Nose walked in on you while you were dumping the powder in a hurry looking for the heroin. He was just looking for a story for his paper. Well, you gave it to him—his obituary. You couldn't take a chance on the snooper queering your play."

"How could I have done it?" Rick interrupted. "I was making a speech in the center of the room when he was killed . . . I don't hear you?"

"I hear you pretty good," Mickey answered. "Where does it say he was killed *during* your speech? He was killed *before* your speech. As soon as you dipped the scissors in his chest, you brushed your suit, cleaned the powder off your shoes and rushed into the living room and asked for everybody's attention. A fast diversion. You wanted it to look like he was killed while you were *on*. That's why you sent Dan into the den looking for the plaque. You wanted him to discover the body while you were talking."

"You're nuts," Rick said with a false bravado. He was trying to act like it meant nothing. But his heart wasn't in it.

"You were the only one who could have done it," Mickey said, summing it all up. "You had the motive and the opportunity. You were in Hong Kong with June and Dan when they met Kim. You knew about June's powder collection. In fact, it was you who publicized it. It was you who were in Hong Kong recently and sent the box of heroin.

"It was you who knew everybody Kim was blackmailing. You told me about them yourself. Except it was you who were setting it all up. You knew she couldn't have done it by herself. It was you and you alone who knew about the nude pictures.

"Furthermore, I happen to know that the boys are not exactly happy with you. You screwed them out of three million bucks. Now they know you have been a little hungry and did a little blackmail business on your own. Maybe they think you got too cocky and decided to keep the stuff for yourself. Take my advice and get yourself locked up in a nice cozy jail. The boys don't like you anymore."

"They can all go to hell," Rick blurted out. "They're not going to make a sieve out of me. I'm not going to be a patsy for them. Everything I did, I did under orders. If I hadn't they would have killed me."

"Are you ready to talk now?" Lieutenant Lodge said coldly as he put his hand on Ransom's shoulder.

"Yes, I'm ready to talk. I'll name names. I'll tell you everything. I'll bust the mob wide open. Only just make sure I'm protected. I'll make a deal with you."

"Ransom," Lodge said as he took him under the arm and hoisted him up, "you're through dealing. Let's go."

It was twelve midnight. June, her mother, Mickey and I were sitting around the kitchen table celebrating with a dozen bottles of Diet-Rite cola. Everybody else had gone home to lick their wounds.

"You were beautiful," Belle said to Mickey. "But tell me, how did you know about the mob being angry at Rick and that they were out to get him?"

"I didn't know. But he didn't know I didn't know."

"And the key to Kim's apartment? How did you know about that?" June asked.

"I didn't," Mickey smiled. "At least I wasn't sure. It just sounded natural. Followed a pattern. When Lodge called me a few minutes ago and told me they found the key on him that fits Kim's apartment, I was just as surprised as you were."

"I'm still in shock," I said. "A lousy box of powder causing so much trouble."

"Yes," June interrupted. "Say, I wonder what happened to that box of powder?"

"Talking about powder," said Belle, powdering her nose, "this is the cheapest stuff you ever had. It doesn't stick to my nose."

"If you don't like it, don't go shopping in my closet," June ribbed. "It wouldn't hurt you to go to a store and put out some hard cash once in a while, you know."

"Why should I?" Mom answered. "I've got a rich son-in-law. Didn't you tell me he's the Catch of the Year?"

"Where did you get that powder?" Mickey asked, taking the compact from her.

"From June's dressing table, where else?" She yawned nonchalantly. "She's got dozens and dozens of boxes of powder. What's one more or less between mother and daughter? But I had to pick this cheap box."

"This cheap box," Mickey said, "is worth about three million. You just powdered your nose with about ten grand."

Mrs. Masters did what any sensible woman would do in her place. She passed out.